KB188159

목탁귀

An Ear to Moktak's Knocking

한영상성시집
목탁귀

1판 1쇄 펴낸날: 2025년 3월 1일

지은이: 양균원
펴낸곳: 독립출판 시걸리
등록번호: 217-28-64436
등록일자: 2024년 12월 24일
주소: (06057) 서울특별시 강남구 언주로 146길18, 5-1302
이메일: sigulli@naver.com

ISBN: 979-11-990904-0-8 (03810)

값 15,000원

목 탁 귀
An Ear to Moktak's Knocking

양 균 원

Kyoonwon Yang

독립출판 시걸리
Sigulli Books

시인의 말

산에서 숲이 내려오고 있다
돌아올 자는 어떻게든 돌아오는가 보다

A Word from the Poet

The forest is descending from the mountain;
Whoever would return seems to find their way back
somehow.

목탁귀

돌은 모로 눕는다
여기도 아니고 저기도 아닌 어디론가
등지고 마주하는 어딘가
다시 그 이후로 돌아눕는다
그러다 꿈쩍없이 구른다
천년을 박혀서 만년을 구른다
모래시계에 갇히는 때가 있으나
저녁 무렵 금모래는
바다를 들어 올리고 있다
구석진 곳 어딘들 박혀 있으나
가두리 없는 산야를 횡단하고 있다
멈춰 선 돌은 없다
어디론가 향하고 있다
있는 그 자리에서
감내할 수 없는 자전의 진동으로
두드리라 스스로 명한다
한결같이 똑 또르르
동백잎에 층층이 굴러떨어져
날이 새는 목탁 소리
들리지 않을 것을 아는 듯 모르는 듯
내색 없이 새벽 산길에 내리박혀
천년을 두드린다
만년을 구른다

An Ear to Moktak's Knocking

A stone lies on its side—
Facing away yet facing,
Neither here nor there, but somewhere,
Turning itself before and after.
Then it flips over without a twitch,
Embedded for a thousand years,
Rolling for ten thousand.
The golden sands raise the sea at dusk,
Though caught in an hourglass at times.
It traverses unfenced mountains and fields,
Though wedged in a certain secluded corner—
No stone stands still; all head somewhere.
Right on the spot, wherever it might be,
It commands itself to knock,
To the very unbearable vibration of self-rotation,
Consistently—tok, tok—
Falling down layer by layer on camellia leaves.
The Buddhist moktak spreads its rappings along the
     valley,
As if it knows it won't be heard, as if it doesn't.
Impassively stuck in the mountain dawning,
It strikes for a thousand years;
It rolls for ten thousand.

목 차
Contents

2. 흐리고 바람 부는 날은
II. When It's Cloudy and Windy

3. 찻물 식어가는 소리
III. The Sound of Tea Cooling

4. 그늘 한 칸의 골상학
IV. Phrenology of a Shaded Haven

1부
커피 한 잔과 사과 한 톨의 라르고

시는 삶의 어느 특별한 세부가 아주 오랫동안 생각되어온 나머지 생각이 그것의 분리할 수 없는 한 부분이 되어버린 것이거나 아주 강렬하게 느껴진 나머지 느낌이 그 안에 들어가 있는 어떤 것이다.

—월리스 스티븐스, 《필요 천사》, 65

I

Largo in a Cup of Coffee and an Apple

A poem is a particular of life thought of for so long
that one's thought has become an inseparable part
of it or a particular of life so intensely felt that the
feeling has entered into it.

—Wallace Stevens, *The Necessary Angel*, 65.

바질

문밖이 소란하다
유—, 내 허락 없이 자르기만 해봐—
여기서 문은 옛 구옥 철문이 아니고
잠금장치가 달린 아파트 현관문도 아니다
바로 내 방문 밖에서
엄마의 생애와 딸의 일생이
내가 날마다 직면해야 하는 현실의 두 세부가
그러니까 얘가 되어가는 마누라와
세상 다 아는 것 같은 강생이가
쟁쟁 맞붙고 있다
다시 조용, 늘 그렇듯 싱겁게 끝난 것일까
올봄 화분에서 웃자란 바질은
식탁 인근에서 어떤 운명을 맞이할까
간헐적 단식에서 오전 11시는
하나, 돌멩이가 가라앉고 있다
두울, 가라앉아 어딘가 박히기 직전이다
토마토소스가 파스타면과 뜨겁게 달아올라
세상의 모든 틈새를 집요하게 파고드는
오, 무염(無厭)의 욕망이여

Basil

There's a commotion outside the door.
"Hey—, don't even think about cutting it!
I want it to keep growing."
This isn't the old iron gate from my boyhood house,
Nor the front door of a locked apartment.
It's just outside my room,
Where a mother's lifetime and a daughter's presence—
Two forces of reality I confront every day—
Collide: a nagging woman turning childlike,
And a know-it-all little monster, cute yet relentless.
Then, quiet again. Did it end blandly, as usual?
What fate lies ahead for the overgrown basil
From this spring's flowerpot by the dining table?
During my intermittent fasting, 11 a.m. becomes:
One, a stone sinking.
Two, sinking deeper, almost lodging somewhere at the
    bottom.
Tomato sauce simmers with the pasta,
Reaching into every crevice of the world.
Oh, insatiable desire.

소띠 그대

느지막이 고운 꽃은
어쩐지 그 이름을 부르기가 힘들다
켜켜이 쌓인 자취를
한갓 명칭이 어찌 불러낼 수 있을까?
호명하면 아니 들은 듯
담담한 몸짓 주변에
희고 붉고 노란
아우라가 아른거린다
아침 마파람에 기대어 술렁이는
나긋한 꽃대가
뫼비우스의 시간을 시소 태운다
저 아랑곳없는 여백에 실려
먼 산 능선마저 잠자리 날개를 편다
희끗 불긋 누릇한
궤적이 아다지오를 지휘하는 시월
바람은 기슭에서 빨라지지만
우리는 기슭에서 느려질 뿐
곁에서 흘겨본다
플라타너스 블라인드 사이 어른거리는 햇살로
내내 단장 중인 소띠 그대
희끄무레 불그죽죽 누르스레한
얼룩이, 혹 봉오리가
소스라치게 맺히고 있다

엄마, 자네, 여보
그따위 통칭의 얼개에서 모질게 빠져나와
갓 터지려 입술을 삐죽 내미는
천년의 딸

You, Born in the Year of the Ox

Flowers in their late bloom,
Their names somehow hard to utter.
How could mere names possibly evoke
Traces layered over time?
When I call them, they seem not to hear,
Remaining tranquil, surrounded by a flickering
Aura of white, red, and yellow.
A flower stem, leaning on the morning breeze,
Teeters Möbius-like time on a seesaw.
Even the distant mountain ridges,
Riding upon an indifferent expanse,
Unfurl their dragonfly wings.
In October, when reddish, whitish, and yellowish
Traces conduct an adagio,
The wind quickens at the seashore;
We slow down only by the riverside.
You, born in the year of the ox,
I glance at you nearby,
Adorning yourself with morning sunbeams
Shimmering through the plane tree blinds.
Spots, or perhaps buds,
Faintly whitened, reddened, and yellowed,
Are forming sharply,

Pouting lips ready to blaze open in a second.
You, late-flowering heart—
Quick! Break free from the frameworks of
"Mother," "Darling," "Honey," et cetera.
For you are a daughter of a thousand years.

요거트

거꾸로 서 있다
냉장고 문짝에 들러붙은
피렌체 베키오 다리
그 곁을 왔다 갔다 하는 눈치더니
주인마님 눈 밖에 난 듯
짧은 목으로
육신을 지탱하고 있다
밖으로 흘리는 땀은 없으나
속에서는 삭은 응유가 고이고 있으리라
저것이 마지막까지 쥔장을 향하는
오체투지의 자세겠지
멋대로 살아서는 곤란하고
사는 대로 살아도 딱하긴 마찬가지고
저 편하자고 드러누워서는
더구나 난감한 일이겠지
아직 남은 체액 마지막 한 방울까지
발바닥이 된 머리끝에 모아
당신에게 바치리라
옛 어른은 요런 걸
단심(丹心)이라고 하겠으나
넌 그저 플레인 요거트 혈통에 따라
생의 끝까지 희멀쑥하게
걸쭉할 따름이겠지

Yogurt

Now it stands upside down,
Supporting its weight on a short neck.
After wandering beside the Ponte Vecchio from
    Florence,
Still glimmering on the refrigerator's door,
The lady appears to have lost her fondness for it.
It doesn't sweat on the outside,
But inside, curdled whey likely pools.
五體投地—five limbs touching the ground:
Forehead, palms, and toes,
This must be the posture of loyalty,
Facing its destiny with wholeheartedness.
Living recklessly brings trouble,
Yet living as instructed feels just as pitiful.
Lying down for comfort
Would be even more problematic.
In a headstand, it gathers its last bit of fluid
At the base—what once was the crown—
Offering the lady even its final drop.
In olden times, this might be called
丹心, devotion of the red heart.
But tracing the lineage of plain yogurt,
You'll finish the day simply—
Thick and pale.

어쩌다 우리는

푸지게 한 상 받았다
미역귀가 바다의 울렁증을 재연하는 동안
지금은 사라진 페인트가 벗겨진 스피커에서
네 박자 스와니강이 퍼졌다
만국기 아래 포크댄스
설렘은 첫에 산다
갑이 자에게 온 것은 어쩌다
을이 축에게 간 것은 저쩌다
그렁저렁하다 소년은 소년을 그만두고
소녀는 소녀를 벗는다
채워지고 비워지고 채워지는
우연의 참화를 딛고 일어선 가문
베이비 붐 세대에 잉태된
밀레니엄 세대가 차려준 잔칫상이었다
눈에는 밟혀도 더는 안 그리운 눈엣가시가
까치 소리로 여는 새 아침
민낯은 어찌하여 텃새의 날갯짓으로
이방 저방을 들락거리는 걸까
미역귀 곰국에 한평생이 출렁인다
우연의 총화가 밥상에 둘러앉아
누구나의 숟가락 젓가락으로
아무나의 그릇에 들락거렸다

경자년의 흰 쥐가 서설을 부른다
공교로운 식구의 오랜 달콤살벌을 기념하여
우리는 내일도 우리일 것이다

How We Came to Be

While a lavish feast was served to me,
The seaweed soup stirred the ocean's nausea once
    more,
And the four-beat rhythm of the Swanee River
Drifted out from a now-vanished, paint-chipped
    speaker.
We danced beneath flags of all nations,
Billowing in the autumn blue sky.
Excitement lives in the very beginning.
It was by chance that A met B,
And another chance that led C to D.
In the course of it all, the boy stops being a boy,
And the girl sheds her girlhood.
Our family rose above the calamity of chance—
Filled, emptied, then filled once more.
The banquet was prepared by the millennial generation,
Born to the baby boomers.
Now, a new morning opens with a magpie's cry.
The thorn in my eye, once a welcome ache in my heart,
Is no longer missed—why does that bare face
Pop in and out of this room or that all day,
Flitting its heavy wings like a sedentary bird?
A lifetime simmers in the seaweed soup on my 60th
    birthday.

A sum of coincidences at the table—
We have dipped into anyone's bowl
With anyone's spoons and chopsticks.
The white rat of 庚子年, the year Gyeongja,
Calls in the auspicious snow.
To honor the long, bittersweet ties of this peculiar
    family,
Tomorrow, we will still be us.

재스민

피고 지고 피는
일 년 내내 바지런한 친구
사진까지 찍어 가슴에 품었다
첫 자줏빛이 탈색해 가면서
앞섶을 하얗게 열어버리는 꽃
그 몸짓이 살짝 헤픈 여자를 상기시켜서
싫다가 좋다가 미워지다가
그냥 친구지 싶어
시큰하게 삭은 마음을 주었다
비좁은 화분에
한 줌 흙을 얹어줄 줄은 알았으나
큰 터전에 옮겨줄 줄은 몰랐다
너에게 어울릴 기후와 토양이
어느 딴 세상에 있으랴
꿈에도 생각하지 못했다
그래도 너는 밤새 새잎을 내밀었다
쓸데없는 데 힘쓰겠다 싶어
웃자란 잔가지를 뚝뚝 끊어 주자
부러진 곳에서 희미한 살내가 풍겼다
그냥 그런 줄 알았다
잎들이 누렇게 변해가도
그러다 하나둘 맥없이 떨어져도
저러다 말겠지 했다
올봄 내내 꽃 소식이 없다

근근이 지탱하고 있다는 듯
한 자세로 고요히 서 있다
창가 바람 새어드는 곳에 옮겨두고
더는 꽃을 요구하지 않겠으니
푸른 기운일랑 잃지 말라고
곁에서 중얼거리고 있다
제발 아프지만 말라고

Jasmine

Bloom, wither, then bloom again—
I have a friend who tirelessly repeats this cycle, year
    after year.
I even took a picture and held it close to my heart.
The flower spread its white lapels wide,
As its initial purple hues began to fade.
Its gestures reminded me of a subtly flirtatious woman,
So I shifted from dislike to fondness,
From disdain to indifference.
Then, thinking, "We're just friends,"
I brought my weary, worn-out heart back to it.
I knew how to add a handful of soil to its cramped pot,
But didn't know how to transplant it into spacious earth.
How could I have imagined
The climate and land for you lay in another world?
I never dreamed of it.
Yet still, you sprouted new leaves overnight.
Thinking it a wasted effort,
I snapped off your overgrown branches.
A faint scent of flesh arose from the broken stems,
But I thought nothing of it.
As the leaves yellowed and dropped, lifeless, one by one,
I believed it would eventually stop.
All spring, there's been no sign of flowers.

As if barely surviving, you remain still in the same
  posture.
I've moved you to a spot where the window breeze slips
  in.
And now I whisper softly at your side,
"I won't ask for flowers anymore, just don't lose your
  green spirit.
Please, just don't get sick."

분가

놓아주지 않는 힘이
미덥다, 거기서 그렇게
껴안고 살았구나, 그래서 사납게
정교하게 가른다, 관계의 틈에
손가락을 집어넣고
헤집는다, 진토를 떨구다가
가까스로 나눠다가
엉킨 속 어디선가, 뚝
불가분은 없다
어둠에 숨어 사는
우리의 뿌리는
누구라는
왜라는 간섭 없이
모두 제각각이기를
그저 무한의 자유이기를
그럴까 소망했으나
하나도 하나가 아니다
얽히고설킨 포옹을
한 몸에 한 뿌리씩
갈라놓는 분갈이의 시간
혼자였다가 여럿이었다가
다시 혼자가 되어가는
풀꽃의 둥지
더러는 외롭게 말라가겠고

더러는 고양이 뒷발에 걸려 넘어지겠지
저러다 어쩌다 너희의 손아귀에서
뒤엉킨 뿌리가 다시 나뉘는 날이 오면
내보낼까 붙잡을까
양가적(兩價的) 욕망이
속절없이 들춰지겠지

A Family into Two

A force that won't let go.
How trustworthy! You lived there,
Embracing so tightly—that's why, so fiercely
And meticulously, I had to split, inserting fingers
Into the crevices of close association,
Prying them apart, shaking off dust.
Then I heard you snap
From somewhere deep within the tangle.
No bond is inseparable.
I wish you could stand self-reliant,
Without interference from who or why;
Yet knowing our roots are blood-bound in darkness,
I wish you endless freedom.
But nothing is truly alone.
It's time to branch out from this entangled grip,
Assigning a root to each body,
Transplanting one family into two or three.
Moment to part—
One to many, and many to one again.
Leaving the nest of wildflowers,
Some will wither in loneliness,
Some will stumble over a cat's hind paw.
And if one day you find yourself in my place,
Facing the chance that tangled roots in your grasp

May split apart like today,
You'll be helplessly drawn into
Ambivalent desires—
Between the will to set free
And the urge to hold on.

문을 열어두고 향을 피우네

거울을 보다 놀란 적 있는가
당신이 아는 당신보다 오래 산
당신을 마주한 적 있는가
지금은 육신을 벗고 어딘들 떠돌고 있을
어쩌면 당신보다 더 당신을 걱정했을 누군가를
목격하고 반가운 적 있는가
그이가 날 보고 있다
냇가에서 등짝을 내밀다가
어깨너머로 슬쩍 흘려보내던 살가운 미소를
상상하고 곱씹은 적은 있으나
저렇듯 두 입 꼭 다물고
응답을 기다려 응시하는 표정을
정면으로 읽어본 적 없다
두 줄 치아를 반듯하게 드러내고 이놈
작게 고함을 들려준 적은 있으나
깊어진 주름 그늘을 하관에 각인하고
호수에 고인 달의 눈빛으로
날 붙잡은 적은 없다
내 안에 내내 살고 계셨나 보다
내 얼굴에 해마다 더 선명해지는 아버지
내일은 동이 트기 전에 대문 앞을 쓸고
모레는 옥상까지 계단 디딤판마다
국화 화분 한 개씩 앉혀놓을 것 같은 그이
거울 속으로 나는 점점 사라지는데

세월의 뒤안길로 떠나간 그이가
내 얼굴을 뚫고 되돌아오는 것은 왜일까
소파에 묻힌 아내의 귀밑에서도
양서방, 나지막이 옆자리에 앉히던
오래 혼자였던 장모님의 흰머리가 비친다
퇴줏그릇에 고인 정종을 음복하는 시간
그이의 까끌까끌한 턱수염이 만져지는 시간
당신은 내 안에 살아왔으나
내가 누군가의 안에 얼마나 살지는 알 수 없으므로
이런 저녁은 흔적 없이 사라질 것이므로
거울 속 당신과의 재회는 그냥 이대로
아름답게 소진되리라

When I Burn Incense
with the Door Open

Have you ever been startled,

Looking into the mirror?

Ever mct someone in it

Who has lived longer than the you you know,

Who cared about you more than you do yourself,

And who might now be wandering without a body?

Have you ever felt joy in such an abrupt encounter?

We face each other through the mirror.

I've imagined and mulled over that warm smile,

Once slyly cast over his shoulder,

As my father offered his back by the swollen stream.

But I have never discerned

His square features, lips sealed tight,

As if anticipating my answer.

Though he has bared two neat rows of teeth

And given me a low, stout call, "BOY!"

He has never captured me with his deep wrinkles,

Shadows etched along his jaw,

Nor with such a moon's gaze reflected in a lake.

My father seems to have always lived within me,

So his face appears clearer on mine every year—

Tomorrow, he would sweep the front gate before dawn,
And the day after, he would place dozens of
    chrysanthemums
On each step up to the rooftop, just like he did in my
    boyhood.
I gradually disappear into the mirror,
And why does he return steadily through my face,
Long after disappearing into the backwater of life?
Around my wife's ear, buried in the sofa,
I catch a glimpse of my mother-in-law's gray hair,
Who, long adjusted to widow's solitude, would quietly
Seat me beside her, whispering, "My dear son-in-law."
I partake of sacrificial drink on my father's anniversary,
And feel the stubble on his chin once again.
He has lived all the time inside me,
But I don't know how long I will inside someone else.
As this night will vanish without a trace,
I wonder if this reunion, too, might fade away,
Simply, but beautifully.

다녀올게

넌 강생이가 아냐
넌 뭐라도 차 내듯
걷는 두 발끝이 모로 향하지
가죽 가방은 엉덩이까지 늘어지고
어깨가 내려온 만큼 턱이 올라가지
넌 더는 강생이가 아냐
고민 같은 것은 털어놓지 않지
실마리가 풀리기 전까지 속 깊이 묻어두지
옛 시절을 들려주면
고통을 음미하듯 재미 삼아 들어주지만
썩 좋아하지는 않지
그래도 넌 내 선택이 무엇이든
그럴 이유가 있을 거라고 믿어주지
아니라면 이러나저러나 상관없다고 느끼는 거겠지
내게 없는 걸 불쑥 사 들고 오지만
뭐가 필요하냐고 묻지는 않지
나라는 존재는 죽 그 자리에 있는 줄 알고
그냥 잘 사는 줄 알고
그런 재주를 동경하는 눈치는 아예 없지만
뭐라 비판하지도 않지
넌 아침 인사도 없고 저녁 인사도 없지
그런 게 전혀 문제가 아니라는 듯
필요할 때 찾아와선 휙 지나가지
넌 그냥 바람이야

그저 겨를 없이 자기 앞의 생과 마주하고 있을 거야
그러다 어쩌다 오늘
아침의 문을 삐거덕 열면서
다녀올게~
그냥 거기 있는 것만으로
충분히 여실한
넌 누구?

I'll Be Back

You're not my little one anymore.
You now walk, turning your tiptoes sideways,
Or carry the leather bag hanging down to your hips,
With shoulders a little slouched, chin raised high.
No, you're not my little one anymore.
You don't share your worries with me,
Keeping them buried deep until the knots come undone.
When I tell hard times from the old days,
You listen, savoring my pain as if it's amusing—
Though not truly enjoying it.
Still, you seem to trust
That there is a reason behind whatever choice I made.
And if not, you just don't seem to care.
You sometimes bring me things I didn't ask for,
But you don't usually ask what I need.
You assume I'll always be here,
Living my life as well as it might be.
And though you don't envy that skill,
You never criticize it either.
You don't greet me in the morning or evening,
As if such things don't matter.
You come when you need something,
And then quickly pass by.
You're just like the wind,

Headlong confronting the life ahead of you.
And then, today,
You suddenly creak open the morning door
And say, "See you in the evening"—
Just your being here
Makes my time so strikingly vivid.

Who are you?

반올림

돌멩이의 낙원
굴러온 것이 굴러간 것 자리에
나앉아 있고 박힌 것보다
뽑힌 것이 더 평화로워요
길 아닌 길
그 마른 천을 걸으면
싹싹한 발굽 소리가 올라와요
물살에 쓸려 한밭을 이룬 정적
걸음을 디딜 때마다 자그락
깨문 입술이 짧게 열렸다 닫히는
파열음이 이어져요
넘어지면 눕고 누우면 뒹구는 자갈이
날 받치고 나아가게 해요
반쯤 무시하면서
슬쩍 수인사라도 건네듯 발목을 당겨요
잠시 남은 자도
먼저 떠난 자 못지않게 닮았으니
내 남루한 발길이 친족의 귀환인 줄 직감했을 터
자잘한 갈망이 둥글게 깨어나 마찰을 전율하는
자갈, 다정하게 함께 걸어요
연푸른 하늘이 땡볕에 타는 공간
큰물 이후에서 하얗게 달궈지는 자갈길을 걸어요
쓸려온 토사에는 야생초가 자리 잡지요
손차양 두른 채 지켜봐요

탁한 물색이 촐랑촐랑 투명해져 가는
그 여름이 어느 여름으로
다시 아무 여름이나로 마구 넘치고
다시 그렇게 말라가는 물살 가장자리에서
홀로 고구마를 심고 있는, 엄니
모든 햇살이 당신을 감싸는 아침에서
모든 그림자가 당신을 호위하는 저녁까지

In a Slightly Sharp Key

A paradise for stones—
What's rolled in has settled
Where what rolled out once lay,
Where the loosened finds more peace than the firmly
    lodged.
I walk across a dry brook, a path that's scarcely a path,
And crisp hooves rise.
A stretch of stillness gathered by the sweeping current,
Each step a quiet crunch—
Like bitten lips, briefly parting and closing,
Tiny plosives echo.
Pebbles that tumble, fall, and roll
Support and carry me forward.
They tug at my ankle,
As if offering a casual greeting, half-ignoring me.
Those left behind are
As worn as those who left before.
Perhaps they sensed my ragged footsteps
As the return of their kin.
Let's walk together for a while, pebbles,
When your small desires roundly awaken, trembling with
    friction.
Under a pale blue sky, scorched by the midday sun,
I walk the sun-whitened pebble road after the flood.

Wild grasses take root in the swept-in silt.
As the murky water turns playfully clear,
I watch and watch, by the water's edge,
Shielding my eyes with one hand,
A summer spilling over into another summer,
Overflowing recklessly into countless summers,
And drying up slowly.
There, I see my mother,
Alone, planting sweet potatoes on the riverbank—
From morning, as sunlight fully surrounds her,
Until evening, as shadows stand guard around her.

커피 한 잔과 사과 한 톨의 라르고

사랑한다는 것은
묵은내가 진동하는 김치냉장고에서
사과 두 톨을 찾아내는 짓
접시 두 개에 나란히 따로 올려놓고
헝클어진 서랍에 숨은
노란 손잡이의 과도를 꺼내 칼날을 벼르는 짓
날마다 사랑한다는 것은
한 알은 여섯 갈래로 등분
다른 하나는 지구의 기울기로 통째 자전시키면서
세월의 한 겹 아침 시간을
드립커피 내려앉는 속도로 깎아가는 짓
차갑고 단단한 속살을 한 조각씩 고백하는
과육의 나열을 다시 배열하는 짓
피아노 협주곡 23번 2악장 아다지오
자연은 신이 만들고 음악은 아내가 만든다
고양이나 개 따위 키워본 적 없어서
핥고 씻어주고 먹여주고 똥까지 치워주고
그런 애정행각은 그저 낯설 뿐이지만
사랑해, 아들 내외에게
문자에 아이콘까지 진하게 쏘았으나
그놈의 사랑이란
누군가에게서가 아니라
지지고 볶아온 세월에서 답을 구해야 할 듯
협주곡 라장조 작품 35번 1악장 알레그로 모데라토

적당히 빠르게 달려온 인생에서 우리는
어쩌다 칸초네타 안단테를 거쳐
혹시 비바치시모 매우 생기 있고 빠르게
정상을 향해 치달을 수 있을까?
커피 한 잔과 사과 한 톨의 라르고
침상에 누워 새해 첫 밥상을 받아들고
아내 왈, 해가 서쪽에서 뜨겠네
왕자 왈, Baby, I'm your man
마님 왈, 그게 대체 무슨 소리야?
서방 왈, 못 알아들었으면 됐어
마눌 왈, 저 노트북 안 되겠네, 고음이 다 깨져
느님 왈, 스피커 따로 사줄까?

Largo in a Cup of Coffee
and an Apple

To love is

Finding two apples

In a kimchi refrigerator reeking of musty days,

Placing them separately on two plates,

Taking out the yellow-handled knife

Hidden in a messy drawer and sharpening its blade.

To love daily is

To slice one apple into six parts,

And to peel the other whole, spinning it as slanted as

the earth,

As if paring a thin layer of morning hours,

No faster than the pace of dripping coffee,

And to rearrange those bare pieces,

Hearing them confess their cold, dense solidity, one by

one.

Piano Concerto No. 23, Second Movement, Adagio.

Nature is made by gods; music by wives.

Never having raised a cat or dog,

Acts of affection like licking, washing, feeding,

Even cleaning up their mess

Are unfamiliar to me.

And I, too, have sometimes sent larger-than-life

emoticons

To my son and daughter-in-law,
With capitalized words: I LOVE YOU!
Yet as for that damn elusive love,
I must say we should seek answers not in someone else,
But in the years of highs and lows we've traversed.
Concerto in D major, Op. 35, First Movement, Allegro
    moderato.
In a life where we've moved at a moderate pace,
After somehow passing through Canzonetta Andante,
Could we yet dash to the peak,
Vivacissimo, lively and swift?
Largo in a cup of coffee and an apple—
Receiving the first meal of the New Year, lying in bed,
House Keeper says, "The sun must be rising in the west."
Prince Charming says, "Baby, I'm your man."
Nagster says, "What on earth does that mean?"
Buddy says, "If you didn't get it, it's fine."
Melodist says, "That laptop won't do, the high notes are
    broken."
Angel says, "Shall I buy you a separate speaker?"

2부
흐리고 바람 부는 날은

세계에서 떨어져 나온 하나의 고립된 사실은 시인에게 아무
런 의미도 없다. 한 사실은 자신의 중요성을 그것이 속해 있
는 현실에서 끌어낸다.... 현실은 사물이 아니라 사물의 양
상이다.... 어떤 사실도 헐벗은 사실이 아니며 어떤 개별적
사실도 그 자체로서 하나의 세계이지 않다.

―월리스 스티븐스, 《필요 천사》, 93, 95, 96.

II
When It's Cloudy and Windy

An isolated fact, cut loose from the universe, has no significance for the poet. It derives its significance from the reality to which it belongs.... Reality is not the thing but the aspect of the thing.... No fact is a bare fact, no individual fact is a universe in itself.

—Wallace Stevens, *The Necessary Angel*, 93, 95, 96.

자지 않는 새

수직 파산으로 생명을 선포하는 소리의 나락
새벽 한 시의 텐트에 빗물이 떼를 지어 생환 중이다

내홍을 불사르던 초저녁 장작더미는 잿가루마저 씻겨 나갔다

자지 않는 새가 있다
두견새와 소쩍새 사이 어딘가에서
불면의 울음소리가 바닷가에 낭자하다

만(灣)에 갇힌 물
곁을 지키는 해안도로 불빛
삶의 테두리를 따라
더러는 이빨 두셋 빠진 잇몸처럼
더러는 수명이 다해가는 손전등처럼
에둘러 명멸하는 한 가닥 영(零)의 행렬
눈먼 바다 위 애먼 하늘 아래
두 쪽 적막을 꿰매는 이음매 솔기로
가라앉을 듯 떠 있다

빗물이 두드리는 법고(法鼓) 속에서
천둥소리를 기다린다

가부좌를 틀고 앉은 파락호였다가
빗소리에 환생한 내장 없는 파라오였다가

우주의 광란이 귀로 들어와 눈으로 나가는 사월의 끝자락에서

식은 모주(母酒)처럼 들쩍지근 깔리는 흰 라일락 향

A Sleepless Bird

In the abyss of sound, proclaiming life through vertical
crashes,
Raindrops come back to life, returning in droves to the
tent at 1 a.m.

The bonfire, lit in the early evening, once ablaze with
inner turmoil,
Has even its ashes swept away.

There is a bird that doesn't sleep—
An insomniac's cry drifts along the seashore,
Somewhere between the cuckoo and the scops owl.

Water trapped in the bay,
The lights of the coastal road, standing guard over their
neighbors,
Tracing the edge of life—
Sometimes like gums with a few missing teeth,
Sometimes like a flashlight, nearing the end of its
battery.
A procession of zeros, flickering and fading,
Hovering as if to sink, stitches together the two halves of
silence,
Beneath the aimless sky, above the blind sea.

I wait for thunder
In a Buddhist drum, beaten by raindrops.

Once a rogue, sitting cross-legged in a lotus position,
Now a Pharaoh, emptied of his insides,
Reincarnated by the sound of rain.

At the end of April,
Where cosmic turmoil enters through the ears
And exits through the eyes,

The scent of white lilacs spreads,
Heavy and dull, like raw rice wine cooling off.

산마루에 호수가 산다

널 안쪽에 두고
빙 돌아 걷고 있다
내가 에워싸는 테두리에서
너의 뜻은 멈춘다
만이 있고 곶이 있어도
늘 너의 바깥쪽에서 걷고 있다
바람이 불어오나 찾아온 것은 아니다
바람이 그쳤으나 떠난 것은 아니다
물결에 하늘이 출렁인다
호수라고 품기만 하는 것은 아니리라
네 안으로 사라진다
아래로 내려가는 것은
잔잔한 물이랑으로 소식을 전하다가
영원히 잠적할 것이다
널 옆에 두고 걷고 있다
이러다가 나 혼자
혹은 너 혼자일 것이다

A Lake Nestles
on the Mountain Crest

I walk around you.
Your significance comes to a halt
Along the boundary I trace.
There are bays and capes,
But I always remain outside the waterfront.
The wind blows, yet never arrives.
The wind ceases, yet never departs.
The sky ripples in the waves.
A lake doesn't merely hold what's inside—
They dissolve into you.
What descends will bring news,
With murmuring waves,
Then vanish forever.
I walk beside you.
At some point, it will be just me,
Or just you, left alone.

강물이 말라야 강바닥이 드러나지

아득히 먼 듯해도
길은 언제나 발밑에 있지
발바닥의 접점을 따라 묵묵히 걷는 것
이것이 운명의 지침이겠으나
길 위에 서성이다가
길 밖에 떠 있는 그들을 본다
저만한 근처에서 저만하게 지내기를
바랄 뿐이었던 그들
스치듯 지나간 적은 숱하여도
꿰뚫어 볼 작심은 드물었으나
이제 넋 놓고 지켜보고 있다
허공에 너울거리는 수십 송이
바람에 몸을 맡겨
굽히다 펴지고
낮아지다 높아진다
저 꽃짓이 오르락내리락 지휘하는 시월이
나에게서 폭풍을 삭제하고
사막을 재설정한다
풍경의 초기화에서 나에게
어쩌다 다른 길로 사라진 너에게도
광기의 미열이 다시 일어나기를
기웃거리고 있다
샘을 찾는다지만
심지어 샘을 판다지만

시가 시시콜콜 시답잖은 시간이
더는 짖지 않는 그림자와
인적의 가장자리를 굽이친다
내리막 후 오르막에서 내려오는 석양
강물이 말라야 강바닥이 드러나지
길 밖에 널 두고
길 위에 서 있다

The Riverbed Is Revealed
Only When the River Dries Up

Though seemingly distant,
The path is always beneath our feet.
Walk quietly along the meeting points of our soles—
This, I decree as fate.
Lingering on the path,
I see those who drift outside it—
Those whom I only wished to stay near,
Those I passed by countless times,
Yet seldom did I intend to see them clearly.
Now, buried in thought, I watch:
Dozens of flowers wavering in the air,
Submitting to the wind,
Bending and straightening,
Lowering and rising.
October, orchestrated by their rise and fall,
Erases the storm,
And resets the desert within me.
From this initialized landscape,
I wish for the fever of madness to stir again in me—
And perhaps in you, too, who disappeared down
    another path.
We are known to seek a spring,

Even declaring we will dig one.

Yet time, so petty in every detail,

Wanders the edges of human footsteps,

Dragging shadows that no longer bark.

After the descent, the sun sets from the ascent—

The riverbed is revealed only when the river dries up.

You veer off, while I stay on the path.

꽃말에 관한 속말

소낙비가 등 뒤에서
햇살 다발을 짜잔 내밀자
카메라 앞에 자세를 잡는다
시선을 탐하는 시선
세상에 나선 지상의 딸들
맘에 품은 것은 몸으로 드러낸다
정문을 탈출한 자의 프로필이 저럴 듯
꽃의 풀이 풀의 꽃으로
떡갈나무 영토를 건너가는 징검다리가 된다
긴 취관(吹管)이 집적하는
한여름으로 가는 길의 음향과 분노
꽃, 꽃의 깔때기가 빨아들인다
맘을 고하는 몸
남녀노소를 흡인한다
백 가지 묘약에 항체를 지닌 여아만이
유모차 밖으로 나오길 거부한다
세상 모서리의 한가운데서
기타 등등에 일어나는 소용돌이
광장이 휩쓸린다
기울어가는 오후마저 침몰한 후
꽃잎 세 장의 상징 따위는
폐교의 화단에 꽂힌 나무 팻말일 터이니
꽃말은 말끔히 잊고
유월, 오늘은 오늘일 뿐

흰 꽃의 향이 이끄는 대로
나팔관의 축음(蓄音)에 춤출지어다
초여름이어서 그렇고 장마 전이어서 그렇고
소낙비는 언제든 쏟아질 거여서 그렇고
우리의 시간이 그래서 그렇고
만발한 처자(處子)들 와중에
아, 꼼짝없이 갇혀서
유월 어느 오후에

Soliloquy on Floriography

June stretches its bouquet of sunshine
From behind a sudden shower. In that very moment,
They strike a pose before the cameras,
Eyes seeking eyes,
The daughters of the earth, freshly ventured into the
  world—
Hearts revealed through bodies.
Such a profile suits those who have successfully
Worked out their escape plan to pass through the main
  gate.
The grass of flowers grows to become the flowers of
  grass,
Becoming stepping stones for us to cross the oak tree's
  domain.
Long floral trumpets gather
The sound and fury of the path to midsummer.
The flowers, with their funnels, drink it all in.
Bodies confessing hearts,
They absorb everything—young and old, men and
  women alike.
Only the baby girl, armed with immunity to a hundred
  potions,
Refuses to step out of her stroller.
Whirlwinds sweep through the glade,

Occurring now in etceteras,

At the very heart of a quiet corner in the world.

As the tilting afternoon slowly sinks,

Such a symbol as the three-leaf flower becomes

Nothing more than a wooden sign

Planted in the flower bed of an abandoned school.

Forget the language of flowers entirely.

It's June—today is simply today.

Dance to the music stored in these trumpets,

Led by the scent of white flower petals,

Because it's early summer, because it's before the
    monsoon,

Because the sudden rain can fall at any moment,

Because our time is like that.

Ah, helplessly stuck among these freshly blooming
    maidens,

On a certain June afternoon.

아침 식사 직후

설렁탕 해장이 끝나가는
어쩌다 일이 없는 어느 아침에
밥알은 남고 국물은 떠나간 뚝배기 앞에서
안주머니로 손이 가는 때가 온다
심장 가까운 데를 더듬자
목구멍 깊은 데서 올라오는 흡연의 충동
식욕이 채워지고 성욕이 발동하는 즈음에
뭔가 미심쩍은
끝나도 끝난 게 아닌 뭔가
딱 명치끝에 걸리는 딸꾹질에서
그저 숨 쉬고 있을 따름
어쩌면 역설적으로
씩씩하게 전진하는 숨은 용기를 지닌 것일 수도
그렇게 째깍대는 초읽기를 지나서
낱장 포장된 아침의 약속
쾌유를 기원하는 투명 봉인을
탁자 아래에서 해제하는 때가 온다
비닐에 새겨진 연번 61은
그런 아침이 두 달여 지났다는 것
다시 시작될 01을 찾아 또 다른 약속이
잡혀 있다는 알림인데
손바닥에 사탕처럼 구르는
노랑, 하양, 하양, 연두
각진 데 없는 동그라미 셋과

언제든 둘로 갈라질 캡슐 하나가 올망졸망
역류의 위장 속에 침투하려는 어느
아침 식사 직후

Right after Breakfast

The hangover soup nears its end,
On a morning with nothing to do.
I sit in front of the soup bowl—
Rice grains remain, but the broth is gone.
It's time to reach for my inner pocket.
I fumble near my heart,
An urge to smoke stirs from deep within.
Hunger is sated, but desire awakens.
Something uncertain—
Something feels unfinished,
Even though it's over.
Stuck in the pit of my stomach,
I'm barely breathing through a hiccup,
Or perhaps, paradoxically,
I'm hiding the courage to move on.
After the ticking countdown fades,
The morning's sealed dose
Unwraps beneath the table,
Releasing its promise of recovery.
The number 61 printed on the transparent plastic
Marks two months of these mornings,
And another appointment awaits
The fresh start of 01.
Yellow, white, white, light green—

Rolling in the palm of my hand like candy,
Three perfect circles with no sharp edges
And a single capsule,
Poised to split in two at any moment.
All come together,
Ready to invade my gastric reflux,
Right after breakfast.

세 시

누구나 지나간다
누가 지나가도 묘하지 않다
나는 벤치에 앉고
벤치는 길가에 네 발로 서 있다
요구르트는 수다쟁이
엿들어도 그만
안 들려도 그만
사회적 거리에 머문다
엄마의 삼 분의 일 지점에서
갈래머리 딸아이가 일으키는 소동
지하철 계단까지 범람한다
죽 따라갔다 돌아오는 내 시선
후박나무 그늘 밑이지만
오후의 가을 햇살이
고이는 하릴없음을 표백하고 있다
전화해볼까?
아니,
오토바이가 야단스레 엄수하는
족발 배달 같은 것
시간약속이란 때로 그런 거겠지
갓 도착한 할머니가
가장 비싼 칠백 원짜리로
내장을 다독인다
멋대로 건너오는 왕수다 곁에서

미동하던 욕망이
보이지 않는 슬리퍼를 찍 끌고 멀어지는
역전 세 시의 길바닥
꼰 다리를 풀고
자, 허리를 세우면

At Three O'Clock

Everyone walks by—
The act of passing by feels not strange at all.
I sit on a bench,
Standing by the roadside on its four legs.
The yogurt-selling woman is chatty—
Overheard or not, it doesn't matter.
I remain at a social distance.
The pigtail girl, a third her mother's height,
Spills her steps toward the subway stairs.
My gaze follows, then returns.
Though I'm shaded beneath a magnolia tree,
The autumn afternoon light whitens the air,
Bleaching the idleness pooled on the pavement.
Should I make a call?
No.
Appointments are like noisy motorcycles,
Hurriedly delivering a dish of braised pig's feet on time.
An old woman, newly arrived, calms her insides
With a brand-name yogurt—the priciest, still under a
    dollar.
Beside the hum of voices,
Crossing the street without permission,
My faint desire recedes, crawling,
Trailing its slippers along the station's sidewalk.

It's three o'clock p.m.
So I'd rather uncross my legs.
And if I were to straighten my back now—

날개를 접고 하강하는 새처럼

내 앞에 뚝 떨어진
꽃, 그 곁에 쭈그리고 앉는다

누군가 날 기념하여 발길에 헌화하는 것이라면

하오나, 날 가로막은 그대는
여름 햇살에 소스라쳐 몸을 던졌을 뿐이겠지요

왜, 라고 물을 뻔했다
하지만 그 질문의 위험을 너무나 잘 아는 까닭에
마치 숨겨진 나 자신의 발목 지뢰를 밟는 것과 같아서

제주 말차는 쌉쌀하게
초콜릿 부처드는 짭짤하게

노을의 뒷맛은 날마다 다르다

이유를 묻지 않는 것은
내가 언젠가 눈부신 바람에 몸을 맡기듯
그대 역시 날개를 접고 하강하는 새일 것이므로

Like a Bird Folding Its Wings
and Descending

A flower falls suddenly before me.
I crouch down beside it.

If only someone had laid it at my feet in memory of
    me—

But no, you must have flung yourself,
Taken aback by the summer light.

I nearly asked, "Why?"
But I know too well the danger in seeking that answer,
Like stepping onto a hidden mine—a toe popper of my
    own.

Jeju matcha tastes bitter;
Chocolate Bouchard, salty.

The sunset's aftertaste shifts each day.

My reason for not asking why is this:
You must be a bird folding its wings as it descends,
Just as I, too, will one day yield to the glistening wind.

백사장 은빛 속으로

길은 정해져 있고
승차했으니 하차할 것이다
주말의 텅 빈 아스팔트
바닷물이 빠져나간 검은 모래사장에서
교차로가 광배근을 드러낸다
내릴 때가 머지않은 주택가에서
달랑 혼자다
버스에 직각이 앉아 있다
같이 흔들리고 함께 멈추는 여백의 도열
손잡이가 군무를 춘다
매달려 쏠리는 허공의 끈
자리마다 붐비는 아무도 없음
느긋이 앉아 있다
승차하면서 그 전을 묻지 않았듯
하차하면서 그 후를 묻지 않을
등골을 묻고 있다
액자마다 잽싸게 바뀌어 걸리고
상징이 켜졌다 꺼졌다 깜박이는
바깥 풍경의 절벽에서
유리 파도가 반짝인다
낮아지는 하늘까지
끝없이 높아지는 백사장
도도하게 흐르는 은빛 속으로
종아리 드러낸 한 소년이 걸어 들어가는
구부정한 귀가에서

Into the Silver-White Sands

The path is set.
Having boarded, I shall disembark.
The crossroads reveal their latissimus dorsi
On the empty asphalt of the weekend, the dark
Sandy beach where the sea has receded,
In a neighborhood close to my stop.
I am all alone.
Ninety-degree angles sit up in unison;
The rows of seats rock together.
Arms clinging overhead sway in the void,
The swinging straps perform a group dance.
Every seat is filled with no one.
My backbone sinks into the seat.
I won't ask about the future when disembarking,
Just as I didn't ask about the past when boarding.
Each bus window quickly shifts its scene,
Moment by moment,
On the precipice of fleeting views.
Glass waves sparkle and lap.
A boy with his legs bare
Walks haughtily into the silver flood—
From white sands rising endlessly
To the ever-lowering sky.
When I return home,
Hunched.

오후의 목신(牧神)

그곳에 안기고 싶다
오늘은 성공하면 좋겠다
구석 자리의 자투리 시간에서
어쩌면 시작할 수 있다
카페에서 커피를 마신다
이게 목적은 아니다
카페에서 음악을 듣는다
이게 목적은 아니다
카페에서 과제를 한다
이게 목적은 아니다
오후의 소란이 나의 익명을 강화한다
내게 신경 쓰는 이가 없어
점차 나도 나를 신경 쓰지 않는다
그렇게 열리는
작은 신의 공간에서
소파 등받이와 하나가 되어
바람이 도착하는 소리
날아오르는 새 떼
강물에 머릴 감는 노을
왠지, 어딘가에 안기고 있는
네 귀의 나

The Afternoon Pan

To be embraced in that place—
I hope it happens today.
Perhaps it can start from a corner seat during leftover
    time.
Often, I drink coffee in a café—
But it's not the purpose.
Sometimes, I listen to music in a café—
But it's not the focus.
Occasionally, I work on assignments in a café—
But it's not the goal.
The afternoon's noise strengthens my anonymity;
No one cares about me,
And I, too, stop caring about myself.
In a small god's space, gradually looming up,
I meld into the sofa's backrest,
Becoming something other than myself.
It's as if I can feel the wind's arrival,
A flock of birds soaring,
The sunset washing its hair in the river.
And finally,
I find myself embraced by someone—
Somehow, somewhere,
With my ears open in four directions.

기분 좋은 날

코를 풀어 본다
콧구멍이 뻥 뚫려서
들숨도 폐까지 신나게 일사천리
이렇듯 아무 생각 없이 깨어난 백치의 아침에
고혈압이나 어깨결림 따위는
신경 쓸 일 없으렷다
시큰둥한 애인 서넛쯤
이참에 정리하고 새 출발 해야겠다
자, 이대로 훠이훠이 세상에 나서면
정거장 가로수에 시 한 줄 걸리겠다
하늘가에 풀물이 얼룩져 있다
거기 녹슨 잡신에게 손목을 내줄 뻔한
성년의 작두질 그 외양간 언저리가
교차로에 어른거린다
폭풍이 연달아 상륙할 것 같은
기분 좋은 예감
텅 빈 백사장의 정신을
새벽까지 늘어지기 일쑤인 문장으로
잡칠 수는 없으렷다
오랜만에 허파에 잔뜩 바람이 들어가는
이렇게 멀쩡한 아침을
어쩌다 한 번쯤은 무상으로
제공하셔도 큰 탈 없으시겠지요,
먼 데 사시는 하느님

On a Good Day

I blow my nose,
Nostrils wide open,
Breathing deeply, down to my lungs.
In this mindless, innocent morning,
Who would worry about high blood pressure or stiff
    shoulders?
This is the chance
To let go of a few indifferent lovers and move on.
Now, if I step out in this mood,
A line of poetry might hang from the tree near the bus
    stop.
The sky's edge stains itself with a hint of green.
The barnyard, where, on the verge of adulthood,
I nearly gave my wrist
To the rusty blade of a straw cutter and the strange god
    within,
Comes alive and lingers at the crossroads.
A good hunch—a series of storms is on its way.
I won't let the empty mind of beach sands
Be spoiled by tedious sentences dragging on till dawn.
Let me fill my lungs with the fresh wind.
Dear God, who lives far away,
Couldn't you, just once in a while,
Grant me this stone-sober morning
Free of charge?

하산을 미루다

호랑이, 그였다면
지상의 먹이사슬을 따라
짐승의 네 발로 어슬렁거리겠다
호랑이, 그였다면
먹빛 띠무늬가 온몸에 꿈틀거리겠다
집우집주넓을홍거칠황
우주는 집, 집이라는 것
우주에 필시 누군가 산다는 것
그런데 그 우주는 어찌 넓고 거친 것일까
하늘천따지검을현누를황
소년은 누런 땅의 청보리밭에 누워
어찌 외계인을 꿈꾸었을까
정상의 저물녘은
산에 산이 가리고
사이에 사이가 끼어들고
농과 담이 엇갈려 아득히
부정맥이 일고 있다
호랑이, 그였다면
죽어서도 사람의 기를 죽이는
가죽을 남기겠다
몸에 온갖 띠를 두르고
가죽이 볼품없는 나는
이름이나마 지워버릴까 궁리하면서
하산을 미루고 있다

Delay the Descent

If I were a tiger,
I would prowl on four beastly legs,
Tracing the food chain of the earth.
If I were a tiger,
Black-striped patterns would undulate along my body.
宇宙洪荒—those words from school days linger:
They say the universe is a house,
A house someone surely resides in.
But why is that universe so vast, so rugged?
天地玄黃—
The sky above, the earth below: black as pitch, yellow as
    gold—
How did the boy lying in the barley field
Dream of beings beyond this yellow earth?
I see dusk draping peaks upon peaks—
Mountains beyond mountains,
Chasms within chasms,
Lights fading into shades,
All blurring into an age-old arrhythmia.
If I were a tiger,
I'd leave behind a pelt
That humbles the human spirit, even in death.
But, cloaked in this dowdy skin with all its wrinkles,
I wonder if I should at least delay the descent
To erase my own name.

무명초(無名草)

목숨은 하난데
머릴 수도 없이 잘랐다
누가 내 머릴 만지면
언제부턴가 기분이 나쁘다
원장이 머릴 감아주는 오늘
엄니도 아니고 마누라도 아니고
애인은 더욱 아닌 처자가
샴푸하고 린스하고 영양제까지 뿌려준다
아무도 더는 관심을 두지 않는데
잘했다, 쓰다듬어 주는 이가 없고
더 깎아, 윽박지르는 이도 없는데
고불하게 말린 반백의 머릿결이 어울린다고
얼굴 없는 목소리가
티 안 나게 달래준다
저절로 묵언 수행 중
누군가 성긴 머리에 손을 얹는다
졸다가 반쯤 감긴 눈으로
내가 나를 본다
푸른 지구 궤도를 응시하는
데이브 보먼, 흰 케이프를 온몸에 두르고
무중력 유영을 준비 중이다
사르륵 귓가 가위질에
마지막으로 다듬어지는 삐진 머리카락
잘라도 멋대로 다시 자라는 저들

그믐밤 삭발하는 돌중이라면
두 손 합장 후 단숨에 깎아내련만

Nameless Grass

I have only one head,
Yet my hair has been cut countless times.
I feel uneasy
When someone touches my head,
Though I can't recall when it started.
Today, the hairdresser—
Neither my mother, my wife,
Nor my lover—washes my hair:
Shampoo, conditioner, even a nutrient spray.
No one shows interest in my head anymore;
No one strokes my hair, saying "Well done,"
Nor is there anyone left to shout, "Cut it shorter!"
A faceless voice soothes me from behind,
Saying my half-white curls suit me.
Someone lays a hand on my thinning hair.
As if lost in meditation,
With half-open, drowsy eyes,
I see my reflection in the mirror—
Clad in a white cape, ready for zero-gravity drifting,
Like Dave Bowman gazing at Earth's blue orbit.
I hear a gentle snip near my ear—
The last rebellious strands are trimmed away.
This nameless grass will regrow as it pleases.
So, with my hands together in prayer,

I wish I were a monk on a dark moon night,
Able to shave it all off without a single stop.

스무고개

난 저 푸른 하늘을 나는 말 궁둥이에 박차를 가하는 자예요
그렇다고 날개 달린 페가수스의 주인은 전혀 아니지요
무한을 횡단하자면 휘발성 광기가 필요하지만 내겐 턱없이 부족
하죠
나의 생존은 불활성 무기력에 피스톤 운동을 일으키는 서탄소 내
연기관 덕이에요
현자도 아니고 지사도 아니고 용자도 아니고 천치도 아닌 나는
제대로 날지 못하는 자들과 함께 숲 근처에 살아요
여름 한 철 땅속을 기어 나와 허물을 벗고 악다구니를 쓰기도 하
지요
육두문자로 밤샌 적 있으나 다시 제풀에 놀라 자지러져요
내게는 세상사 강물처럼 둥실 실어 보내는 우공의 눈동자가 없어요
거친 잡풀을 삭이고 되새김하는 위장도 없고요
간혹 아이스크림의 황제를 좇아 냉장고 곁을 어슬렁거려요
그래도 쥔장의 흰 손등을 핥는 견공의 혓바닥은 싫어요
노을에 여명을 가두고 풀어주고 가뒀어요
누군가 떠나면서 남긴 어깻짓이 골목 끝에 어른거리는 때가 있어요
나는 타인의 향기가 스쳐 지나가는 카페가 아니에요
붙잡고 씨름하는 문장에는 지우고 닦아도 내 살내가 짙지요
신을 찾을 때마다 신이 사라지는 꿈에서 맨발로 경공술을 펼쳐요
닳지 않은 사랑을 달지 않게 담그는 은유를 구하고 있어요
나는 말라가는 감귤 껍질 옆의 다초점 안경이 아니에요

한잔의 커피와 혈압의 상관관계를 기억하는 관리 수첩도 아니고요

쇠가 아닌 탓에 흙처럼 유하지 않고 물이 아닌 탓에 불처럼 뜨겁지는 않은

햇빛의 기울기로 달빛의 상승을 응시하는 느티나무 아래에서

이도 저도 아닌 나는 과연 누구인가요?

Twenty Questions

I am the one who drives the horse soaring through the
  blue sky,
Yet I am not the master of winged Pegasus.
To traverse infinity, we need volatile madness, but I am
  sorely lacking it.
I owe my survival, through inert lethargy,
To a low-carbon engine that sluggishly stirs pistons to
  life.
I am neither a sage nor a patriot nor a hero nor a fool.
I live on the edge of the forest, among those who cannot
  fly well.
In summer, I crawl up from underground, shedding my
  skin, sometimes screaming aloud.
Some nights, I stayed up hurling curses, only to be
  startled by my own voice and fall silent.
I lack the large eyes of a calf, calmly letting worldly
  matters drift downstream,
Nor do I have the stomach that digests rough weeds,
  then ruminates.
At times, I loiter around the refrigerator, chasing the
  emperor of ice cream,
But I dislike a dog's tongue that licks its owner's pale
  hand.
I locked dawn within the sunset, released it, then bound
  it once more.

At times, a departing shoulder's shrug lingers at the
    alley's end.

I am not a café where others' scents drift past;

The scent of my flesh lingers thickly in the sentences I
    wrestle with and revise.

In a dream where God vanishes whenever I seek Him,

I practice flying with inner strength on bare feet.

I search for a metaphor that can hold undiminished love
    without turning too sweet.

I am not multifocal glasses, lying beside a drying
    tangerine peel,

Nor am I a health journal tracking the link between
    coffee and blood pressure.

I am neither soft like soil, for I am not iron,

Nor hot like fire, for I am not water.

Under a zelkova tree, watching moonlight ascend as
    sunlight tilts,

Caught between here and there—

WHO AM I?

내가 나를 보듬는 날

창가에 기댄 시선이
나비 날갯짓하는 아침이 있네
트로트 가사에 물큰해지고
삼시세끼가 진저리쳐지는 무량한 수렁이네
물색이 좀 더 흐릿해지면
진창의 속살이 욕망을 드러내겠네
십 리를 감싸도 안개는 제자리에 술렁일 뿐이네
소 혓바닥 점액이 핥고 지나가는 정수리 신경 다발
젖혀지고 뒤집혀 더 멀리 더 깊이
미립자의 전율에 미끄러져 휘말리듯
엇나간 시간이 빗나간 시간과 자웅동체를 이루는 때가 있네
나도 모르게 내가 나를 껴안네
은은하게 살아있다고
탄 맛에 신맛이 감도는 블랙이어서 괜찮다고
짧고 강하게 코를 풀어보네
엄지와 검지가 오르락내리락 콧잔등을 문질러대는
외면과 대면하는 국면이 오면
언제 떠난 적 있느냐 곁을 지키고 있는 그림자의 혜량
찾지 않았는데 부르지 않았는데
알맞게 늙은 얼굴을 내미는
당신의 저체온 같은 그런 무탈한 환장이 있네
수평으로 돌아가는 자전의 각도
십 리 뻘밭 너머 저편에
성년의 돌팔매가 소리 없이 내려앉네

쓸개 터지지 않게 애를 다루는 방식
오늘의 저녁 식단은
기억의 짚단에 싸여 심층까지 삭은
홍어 삼합일 것
이렇듯 쓴 신맛에 암모니아 향이 콧속을 후비는
세상 언저리를 맴돌다가 어느새 어둑한 시장 골목이면
고향 떠나 출세한 장흥 촌놈을 소환하겠네

When I Embrace Myself

Some mornings, my gaze leans against the window,
Fluttering like butterfly wings.
They are the very mire in which I am intoxicated
By trot song lyrics and grow weary of the three-meal
    routine.
As colors fade, the mire's flesh reveals murkier desires.
Even when mist envelops for miles,
It simply stirs in place.
The nerve bundle at my crown,
Licked by a cow's mucous-covered tongue,
Tilts, overturns, and slides deeper into quivering
    particles.
These are the moments when swerving times
Merge with digressing times, forming a hermaphrodite.
Unknowingly, I embrace myself,
Whispering, "Stay alive with a soft glow,"
As the burnt bitterness of black coffee makes it
    bearable.
I blow my nose with a short, strong breath.
When my thumb and index finger slide up and down the
    bridge of my nose,
Distorting a face that turns from what I've faced,
Your shadow offers limitless solace,
As if it has never left my side.

Unbidden, it appears in a harmless frenzy,
A suitably aged face, like your cool body.
My axis rotates horizontally.
The stone I cast in adulthood quietly settles
Beyond the muddy field.
Careful attention to a skate liver,
As one might handle a gallbladder to prevent it from
    bursting.
Tonight's dinner might be a mix of kimchi, pork, and
    skate,
Fully fermented in the straw of memory.
When darkness falls over the market alley,
Hovering at the world's edge,
Where bitterness, sourness, and ammonia pierce tongue
    and nose,
I will summon the country boy from Jangheung,
Who once left home and carved his path in the world.

흐리고 바람 부는 날은

컷,
흐리고 바람 부는 날은
순서가 사라져 좋다
컷,
다들 수고했어요
초점 밖에서 걸어오는 이들
태연하게 스쳐 갈 줄 아는 이들
주인공은 없다
흐리고 바람 부는 날은
이름 없고 대사 없는 엑스트라들이
배경에서 걸어 나온다
개망초 세상에는 아, 처음도 끝도 없어라
누군가의 중심이 사방에 뿌려진다
어디서든 어떻게든 흔쾌히 살아가는 이들
가도 가도 끝없는 망초, 망초, 개망초꽃은
바람 센 물가 언덕에 흐드러지게 흩어지고 있다
능소화 홍조가 시선을 끌어도
망초, 망초, 개망초는 욕망도 없고 울분도 없이
애인이 없어도 그만이라는 듯
날 쓸고 널 닦고 하늘길을 열고 있다
흐리고 바람 부는 날은
너는 네가 아니라고 나는 내가 아니라고
다 같이 자신을 부정해도 좋으리라
앞을 부인하고 뒤를 거부하고

나는 너에게 너는 그에게 그는 누군가에게
그저 그만그만한 날
흐리고 바람 부는 날은
순서가 없어 좋다
망초, 망초, 개망초꽃 언덕길을 걷는다
이미 늦은 듯 느긋하게 걷다가
흔들리고 무뎌지고 번져가다가
시원하게 비 쏟아지기 직전의 탁한 여백 속으로
컷, 나긋나긋 묻혀가는 형상이기를

When It's Cloudy and Windy

Cut,
When it's cloudy and windy,
It's nice that no order overwhelms.
Cut,
Well done, everyone!
They step in, emerging from a blur,
They know how to drift by, nonchalant.
There is no lead among them.
When it's cloudy and windy,
Extras come forth from the backdrop—
Thousands of fleabanes flooding the banks,
Neither beginning nor end.
There, you may see your ego set free on all sides.
They're ready to settle anywhere.
Fleabanes, fleabanes, endless, voiceless,
Drift along the windy riverside hill.
Even if the orange trumpet vine's blush catches the eye,
Fleabanes, fleabanes, daisy fleabanes—
They stand alone, free of desire or resentment,
As if they don't mind living without a lover.
Sweeping me, brushing you,
Carving a path toward the sky.
When it's cloudy and windy,
It's fine if you deny yourself, and I, myself,

As everything now shakes its head.
Turning away from both front and back—
I to you, you to him, he to another.
Just ordinary, nothing special—another day.
When it's cloudy and windy,
It's nice that no single color stands out.
I walk and walk into the fleabane-covered hill,
Leisurely, as though already late,
Swaying, dulling, spreading.
Cut—into that hazy blankness,
Just before a sudden shower pours down.
If only you could see my lithe form slowly fading away.

3부
찻물 식어가는 소리

앞선 생각이나 뒤이은 생각 없이 사물 그 자체를 오직 매우
뛰어난 지각력으로 바라보시므로, 내 어머니는 ⋯ 대단한
상상력을 지닌 분이다.

　　　　　　　　　　　　　−윌리엄 칼로스 윌리엄스, 《평론 선집》, 5.

III

The Sound of Tea Cooling

[S]eeing the thing itself without forethought or afterthought but with great intensity of perception, my mother ··· is a creature of great imagination.

—William Carlos Williams, *Selected Essays*, 5.

당신이라는 환유

뜨거운 환호
갓 내린 커피 한 잔이
당신의 은유(隱喩)에 엎질러졌다
지면에서 지면으로
먼저 달아오른 지점을 따라
콩 볶은 탄내가 막장까지 젖어든다
갈색으로 부풀어가는 지층이
땀인지 눈물인지 터져 나온 신음까지
몸에 새기는 현장
모로 쓰러진 머그잔이
돌아누운 행간에게 내미는 입술
자세를 유지하고 제때 물러서던
당신이 속절없이 흔들린다
간헐천이라도 곧장 치솟을 듯
뒤틀린 어느 화산지형에서
당신의 온유한 환유(換喩)는
폭발 직전의 응축이 안전밸브를 열고
간간이 내뱉는 물기둥일까
관계의 접점마저 다듬어져 가려지는 때는
바람의 저쪽으로 머쓱하게 흩어지는
그러다 허공으로 화하는
물 가루일까
서서히 말라가고 있다
비뚤어져 돋아나는 지상의 활자

귀퉁이로 갈수록 더 거세게 너울거린다
혹이 돋은 문장의 줄기
낱장의 뿌리가 서로 얽히고 있다
한동안 우리는 웅크릴 것이다
커피 한 잔을 끝장까지 내리고
쓴맛 신맛 간혹 고소한 맛
시간의 근육음(筋肉音)이 먼지 올처럼
오후 창가에 맴돌 때까지

You, Whom I Call Metonymy

Hot cheers—
A freshly brewed cup of coffee
Just spilled over your metaphors!
From paper to ground,
Following the points heated earlier,
The smell of roasted beans permeates to abysmal
    depths.
Sweat or tears, even burst-out groans,
Etch themselves into the body's strata, swelling brown.
The mug, fallen on its side,
Offers its lips to the space between lines, rolling onto
    their backs.
You, who maintained your posture and withdrew at the
    right time,
Now helplessly shaking,
As if a geyser would shoot straight up
In a certain twisted volcanic terrain.
You, whom I would call gentle metonymy—
Are you a column of water, sporadically exhaling
As the safety valve opens just before the explosion?
Or are you water vapor,
When the contact points of relationships, refined and
    blurred,
Scatter awkwardly to the other side of the wind

And dissolve into the void?
Drying up so gradually,
Your letters stand out on the crooked ground,
Swaying more violently around the corners.
Bumpy sentences raise their heads,
And every page's roots entangle.
For a while, we will crouch in this pause,
Brewing a cup of coffee to the very end,
Until time's muscular sounds taste
Bitter, sour, or occasionally savory,
Hovering like a few strands of dust
Near the afternoon window.

금악행(琴岳行)

바람의 이쪽
씨앗이 날아갔고 이삭이 부러졌고
내장을 비운 미라가 떼지어 기립하는 능선
너희를 너희라고
누구도 더는 알아차릴 수 없다
속 빈 풀대가 무성하다
나이테가 없는 너희는 필시
새 떼가 어딘들 앉았다 떠나가듯이
문득 지나가고 있을 터
아직, 오름 마루에 버티고 있다
볍씨를 틴 볏단은 타작마당에 눕기라도 하지
북서풍 너울에 속속들이 일렁이는 깡마른 줄기들
그 자리에 있어야 할 이유를 잊은 채
색도 향도 날려 보내고
일몰의 등고선을 지키고 있다
강철의 빗살무늬가 바람길을 쓸고 있다
너희 씨족은 억새였을까
지대공 전선에 배치된 풀, 풀
서슬 푸른 칼날도 창공을 찌르던 창도 잃었다
맨손으로 막다가 손가락이 부러졌고
그마저 덜렁거리다 날아갔다
상처가 아물기 전에 끊어진 상처
물마저 서쪽으로 달아나는 중산간에서
청춘을 소환해줄 모든 것을 잃고

112

종(種)의 기원을 잊고
이름마저 벗고
이승에는 더 없을 순수한 껍질로
내 앞에 환하게 회초리를 쳐드는
무명의 너희

Journey to Geumak,
the Volcanic Cone

On this side of the windy ridge,

Where mummies stand in groups, devoid of guts,

Seeds have blown away, grains broken off,

No one can recognize you as you anymore.

Hollow stems grow profusely,

With no growth rings to show,

You must be passing by unexpectedly,

Like a flock of birds,

Perching and taking flight anywhere, anytime.

Still, you stand at the crest of the volcanic cone.

While rice sheaves would lie down in the threshing yard,

Your skeletal stalks stand firm on their one-legged
    stance,

Trembling entirely in the northwest wind.

You, guardian of the sunset's contour,

With no reason to stay in place,

With no color or scent left,

For what do you sweep the wind's path with steel
    brooms?

Were your ancestors silver grass?

Grass, a patch of grass, deployed on the earth-to-air
    battlefront,

All the blue-blooded blades and sky-piercing spears are
    gone,
Blocking with bare hands until fingers are severed,
Then the dangling bones fly away,
Then the scars are cut out before they heal.
Even water escapes westward through the mid-mountain
    range.
Whatever can summon youth is lost.
The origin of species forgotten,
Even your name erased,
You, hollow culms, purer than anything in this world,
Raise, raise a bright wave of whipping rods over me!
You, the anonymous.

저 흰 소 떼

오르간 소리가 울린다
그 여진 속에 주임신부가 주님을 울린다
그 여파 속에 갓 나온 매미가
장맛비 잠깐 그친 하늘에 신고식을 올리는 중
나지막이 울음을 터뜨리는 리허설
초하도 그런 중일 것이다
아직 온 힘을 다 쏟을 수 없다
치열하게 증명해야 할 마음을 찾아서
일렁이는 대로 흔들릴 따름
몸 깊이 태풍이 잉태되고 있다
두 개의 악명 높은 비바람 사이에서
배롱나무꽃이 온 연못을 덮는 날이 올 것이다
크게 너를 찾고 짧게 나를 던지는
그런 때가 있다 올 것이다 지나갈 것이다
성당 안이 고요해졌다
매미 한 마리와 새 한 마리
매미 두 마리와 새 한 마리
매미 한 마리와 새 두 마리
저들도 성당 밥을 먹고 사는 족속답게
바닷바람에 지상의 화음을 싣고 있다
느티나무 잎이 일으키는 수천 무음 진동을
부드럽게 쓸고 가는 무심으로

성모상 옷 주름에 하얗게 파고드는 무자비한 땡볕으로
초여름이 척 부챗살 펼쳐놓은
바다 위 저 흰 소 떼

Such a White Herd of Cattle

The organ resonates—
In its echo, the parish priest moves the Lord to tears.
In its wake, the newly emerged cicadas offer
Their debut performance to the near sky,
Where the monsoon rain briefly pauses.
They rehearse their soft cries in a low key.
Perhaps summer, too, is on the same path,
Not yet able to release all its strength,
Still searching fiercely for a proven heart,
Swaying with the coming waves.
Typhoons are being conceived deep within.
The day will come, between two notorious storms,
When crape myrtle flowers will blanket the pond.
On that day, you will seek yourself aloud,
Flinging yourself briefly.
The day will emerge, arrive, and pass.
The cathedral has grown quiet inside.
Cicada one and bird one,
Cicada two and bird one,
Cicada one and bird two—
As if living on the church's benevolence,
They load the sea breeze with earthly harmonies.
Early summer, steadily brooding,
Ready to spread its fan ribs wide,

Softly passes through the zelkova leaves'
Thousands of silent vibrations with its indifferent mind,
Blindly piercing through the Virgin Mary's marble robe
With its merciless scorching beams—
Such a white herd of cattle
Above the distant sea.

지상의 오랜 명사들

녹이 슬고 있다
손톱 뿌리에서 멍이 자라듯
방치의 펜촉에 흰 녹이 번지고 있다
볼펜 똥을 짓이겨 써낸 몇 행도
라일락 나무 밑처럼 그늘이 옅다
길이 길로 이어지는
영원한 자기복제의 저주에 갇혔다
어디서 누구에게 무엇을 구하든
너라는 원점에서 시작하는 나라는 맹점
너를 저장하는 일이 불편해졌다
사이렌이 휘젓고 지나가는 노을의 항적에서
삭제해도 지워도 재생되는 거품들
왜곡에서 불순하게 창조되는 것들
정차했다가 주차했다가
마침내 바큇살부터 녹슬어가는
무수한 너를, 본다
안경 얼룩을 닦는 순간에서
다시 너에게 가는 짧은 길이 열린다
서랍에 처박아둔 붓을 꺼낸다
가늘어서 쉬 달아지는 끝
그 한 줌 세모가 한 점에 모여서 시작되는
너라는 무대 위의 나
갈고 갈아 잔잔한 먹물의 심지로
붓질을 따라가다 보면

마음의 파고가 낮아지겠지
너를 필사했으나 뜻은 다가오지 않고
지상의 오랜 명사들만 흩어진다
획의 몸짓이 되어라
들풀의 어깻짓으로
너를 파자(破字)하다가
나를 해자(解字)할 수 있기를

Long-Standing Words on Earth

Rust is settling in—
White rust forms on the tip of a neglected pen,
Like bruises beneath a fingernail.
A few lines in ballpoint ink, smeared and scrawled,
As shallow as the shade beneath a lilac tree.
I am cursed with the eternal self-cloning
Of one path leading to another.
No matter where, who, or what I seek,
I am always a blind spot, starting from you as the origin.
It has become uncomfortable to store you.
Endless errata—
Those greedy slick bubbles of distortion
Keep returning, even after deletion and erasure
In the wake of sunsets stirred by sirens.
Stopped by occasionally, parked for a while,
And at last, you are left in ruins.
Now I see countless versions of you,
Rusting away from the broken spokes,
Through unlit headlights to the grizzly sky.
A short path to you is about to open again
In the very moment I polish my glasses.
I pull out the brush long buried in the bottom drawer—
Its tip, worn from thin bristles,
Narrows to a sharp point.

I, on the stage of you,
You, always a step ahead of me.
Let me follow the brush strokes,
Let me grind the ink stick to the core of tranquility
Until the mind's waves settle.
As I transcribe you,
The meaning does not come closer,
Yet long-standing words on earth scatter quietly.
Let me mimic the gesture of a stroke,
As a wild leaf does with its oblique shoulder—
If only I could break down your calling, one stroke at a
    time,
Perhaps I could decipher my own.

동행

늦겨울 숲길에는
접혔다 펼쳐지는 것이 있다
진달래가 한창이었다면
등 뒤에서 두 눈을 가려오는
바람의 빈손을 느끼지 못했을 터
두세 시간 뒤따라오다가
어깨에 밀착해오는
까치, 까치를 돌려보낸 후
발길에 탁 차이는
밤송이의 방어기제가 빈속을 뒤집는다
멀리 고이는 것에는 푸른
심도가 자란다
능선에 잠깐 쉬어가는 참에
눈꺼풀은 닫고
부처 귀는 열어두는
허허심처,
헛눈깨비 세상이다
거기서 여기일 것이다
다시 하산 무렵에
세상 소음이 반가운 것은
네 갈래 오이소박이 탓만은 아니리라
국밥이 식어가도 숟가락 꽂아두고
종잇장 귀를 접는 짓
학수고대해도 강림하지 않다가

저 안에서 쑤시듯 아려오는 놈 탓이리라
내 삶의 뒤안길에
보일 듯 말 듯 따라다니는 녀석
깜짝이야, 안녕!

Companion

Walk along a late-winter forest path,
And you'll see something folding and unfolding there.
Had the azaleas been in full bloom,
You wouldn't have felt the wind's empty hands
Blindfolding you from behind.
Squeaky magpies, following me for two or three hours,
Now cling closer to my shoulders.
After sending them away,
I kick at a chestnut burr—
Its defensive armor turns its empty belly inside out.
In whatever resides in the distance,
A deep blue depth grows.
Once given a brief rest on the ridge,
I find myself in a void, free of distractions,
With eyelids horizontally closed,
And Buddha's ears vertically open.
A world of fleeting snow:
Here must be there.
As I descend again,
I'm glad to hear the world's noises—
Not because four-pronged cucumber pickles stir my
    taste,
But because of that companion,
Surging inside, poking and aching,

After denying me long-awaited expectations.

I fold a page's corner in my forget-me-not notebook,

Letting the rice soup cool, the spoon standing alone in
   it.

That elusive figure,

Barely visible, always trailing behind,

On the backward path of my life—

Oh, hello!

나의 신을 찾아서

무중력 외계에서 깼다
커피포트가 우주의 조난신호를 수신한다
색이 사라지면서 은은해지는 물색
난 우주 먼지로 떠 있다
외로움이 그냥 달큼해지는 때가 있다
도심의 수천 창문에 아침노을이 비치면 일어나는 현상
삶은 달걀을 벗기자
둥근 달이 모로 눕는다
다행히 야한 흉터는 없으나
눈 코 입도 없다
잊지 않는데 떠오르지 않아서
기억하지 않는데 떠오르는 것을 고대한다
증상은 원인이 된다
언젠가 바람이 된다
비가 물이 되어 물은 비를 잊는다
잊어야 흐르고 잊어서 흐르고
잊으려고 흐르고 아마 잊지 못해 흐르고
바람이 바람에 헛손짓한다
산은 하늘 아래 있으나
산 위 하늘은 바다에 있다
낯선 신들이 눈치껏 짝짓기를 시도하는
마루 밑에서 굴다리 밑 녹슨 철로 위에서
검정 단화 두 짝이 앞서거니 뒤서거니
그 옆에서 하늘색 교복이 왼발 오른발

외연이 무너져 내연이 세상을 덮치고
나의 신을 찾다가
툇마루 끝에 맨발로 깬다
몸도 마음도 더 나아갈 곳도 다 흐릿하여
어서, 남의 것이라도 훔쳐야겠다

Finding My Shoes

I wake up in a zero-gravity alien realm.
A distress signal from space reaches the coffee pot.
The colors of things fade, becoming subtle.
I drift like cosmic dust.
Loneliness is sometimes simply sweet,
When the morning glow brushes a thousand city
     windows.
I peel a boiled egg; an oval moon lies on its side.
Thankfully, there are no obscene scars,
Nor are there eyes, a nose, or a mouth.
I yearn for what emerges without my recollection,
For I know what does not arise without my forgetting.
Symptoms become causes.
One day, they will become wind.
Rain becomes water; water forgets the rain.
We must forget to flow, perhaps having forgotten to
     flow.
We must flow to forget, perhaps flowing so as not to be
     forgotten.
One wind makes futile gestures at another.
The mountain is under the sky,
And the sky is in the sea.
Beneath the floor, where strange shoes subtly try to pair,
On the rusty railway beneath the overpass,

A pair of black soles alternates in the lead, ahead or
    behind,
And a sky-blue school uniform walks along, left or right.
Denotation collapses; connotation engulfs the world.
Another failure in my search for my soul-mate.
I wake up barefoot on the edge of the worn-out floor,
My body, mind, and destination all blurred.
Hurry up—I'd rather steal someone else's.

별일 없는 나날의 일지

낙엽이 떼지어 날아가요
어스름이 굽이굽이 이부자리를 펴네요
담장 위 빈 깡통을 지나 소용돌이치는
그 너머는 어느새 마지막 계절이에요
민원으로 폐쇄된 흡연장 바닥에
밤새 뿌려진 광고지처럼 납작 엎드릴지
반투명 선글라스를 걸치고
먼 나라 약손 마사지를 탐험할지
숯불 향 어지러운 고깃집 불판 가에서
맥주에서 소주로 세월을 남하할지
골목이 퇴근길 현기증을 일으켜요
일탈의 기술은 통달하기 어렵지만
바람 반대로 기우는 버릇 또한
수리하기 쉽지 않지요
유리에서 유리로 희끗거리는 빛무리
맺혔다 떨어지는 신호
온 데서 와서 간 데로 가는
가로수 직립보행을 따라
빗살무늬가 그어지고 있어요
어때요, 미친개처럼 짖어볼까요
울 듯 말 듯 기대어오는
저 가을비 사선을 향해

Journal of Ordinary Days

Autumn leaves take flight in flocks,

As twilight spreads its bedding at every turn.

Swirling, passing through the empty cans on the brick
wall,

The final season has already arrived, over there.

Shall I lie flat in the smoking area, now closed by
complaints,

Like flyers scattered overnight,

Or don translucent sunglasses

To explore some distant country's healing massage?

Shall I let time drift southward, from beer to soju,

At the grill of a smoky barbecue restaurant?

The narrow alley spins, dizzy with people returning
home.

The art of deviation is hard to master,

But neither is it easy to break the habit

Of leaning into the wind.

Light flickers from glass to glass.

Signals bud and fall—blue, yellow, red.

Faint lines are being drawn

Along the street trees, walking upright,

From where they came to where they go.

How about we howl for a minute, like mad dogs,

At the autumn rain's diagonal lines,
Effortlessly leaning in,
As if on the verge of tears?

나는 날마다 가출한다

소소한 정오가 날마다 다가와서
이런들 저런들 곁을 스치자
바람 쐬러 간다고
한 대 태우고 오겠다고
그렇게 멀리 사라져간 영혼을 찾아
소년은 가출한다, 소녀는 가출한 소년을 찾아 가출한다, 소년은
가출한 소녀를 찾아 출가한다, 소녀는 물가에 남는다
내가 가진 판본은 그러하지만
이게 최종본이라고 주장하는 것은 아니지만
욕조를 비울 때마다
솥 바닥 긁어대는 쇠숟가락 소리가 난다
화병에 꽃이 꽂혀 있지 않다는 걸
대수롭지 않게 인정하는 대청소 날이 오면
당신이 끓여 준 된장국, 당신이 그려준 하트, 당신이 대필한 원
고, 당신이 밤낮으로 접속한 몸의 단축키, 그 무수히 만개한 안개꽃
소수점들이 흔들렸다 지고 쓸리고 치워지는 어느 날 어느 탁자 어느
빈 병 하향 곡선을 따라 한 끼니가 시들하게 미끄러지면
천천히 수직 추락하는 유령이 딱 숨골에 멈추면
화요일 오후, 아니 월요일이거나 수요일, 아니 아침이거나 저녁,
시간의 경계가 사라져 이전도 없고 이후도 없고, 어쩌면 지금도 없
는, 그런 찰나들이 침상에 쌓여 푹신하게 당신을 품는 밤이면
잘 지내고 있다, 다만

I Run Away Every Day

When noon approaches,
Passing by as little things do each day,
And a soul says, "I'm going out for some fresh air,"
Maybe he just meant to take a smoke break, but he's
    gone, never to return.
In search of the one who has disappeared far away,
A boy runs away, a girl runs away to find the boy,
The boy becomes a Buddhist monk to find the girl,
And the girl lingers by the water.
This is the version of my story,
Yet I do not claim it as definitive.
Whenever I drain my bathtub,
I hear a metal spoon scraping the bottom of an iron pot.
If the day comes, after a thorough cleaning,
When I casually accept that there are no more flowers in
    the vase,
If the day comes when the soybean paste soup you
    made, the heart symbols you drew for me, the
    manuscripts you ghostwrote, the contours of my body
    you touched day and night, the tiny, swaying dots of
    baby's breath—all those little details bloom, sway,
    and are swept away,

If another meal blandly slides into my stomach, down
   the curve of a certain empty bottle on a certain desk
   on a certain day, and a slowly sinking ghost comes to
   rest in the pit of my chest,
If there seems to be no before, no after, perhaps not
   even a now, on a Tuesday afternoon—or maybe
   Monday or Wednesday, morning or evening—with the
   boundaries of time erased,
If moments like these softly pile up on the bed,
   embracing me tenderly at night,
I'm doing fine, just ...

모과

목어, 목이 마르다
모과, 절 마당 풍경을 받치고 있는 돌대가리들
저 마지막 밑장이 빠져
세상 모퉁이가 와르르 무너질까
올려다보고 있다
혹시 내 울상을 한 대 후려쳐 줄까
낙과를 기다리고 있다
못났다, 이런 소릴 듣고 자란 놈 치고
실하지 않은 자가 없다
우락부락 걸려 있다
까치 주둥이로는 쪼아댈 엄두를 못내는
응어리가 있다
아무도 말을 하지 않는다
아무도 듣지 않는다
아무도 쳐다보지 않아서
아무렇지도 않다는 듯 자라온 심성일 것
배신, 밤새 몰래 떨어졌다
널 난도질하여 그 미덥지 않은 육즙을 우려낼까
썩게 버려둘까
썩어가는 향이나마 거둘까
성숙해진다는 것은
밋밋하게 맹점이 되어가는 것
까마귀 떼가 날아가는 쪽으로
못 내려온 돌대가리들이

흠칫거리고 있다
바람, 맞아도 싸다
바람, 난 너에게 언제 모과일 수 있을까

Quinces

A wooden fish, thirsty.
Quinces, stones that support the temple yard's scenery.
I look up,
Wondering if the last stone at the bottom might fall,
And a corner of the world collapse with it.
I wait for a falling fruit
To strike my frowning face.
You're a fool! No one is as strong
As one who's grown hearing such harsh words.
They hang, craggy and stubborn.
They hold an unbreakable core—
Even a magpie's beak wouldn't dare peck at them.
No one speaks,
No one listens,
No one looks.
This is how they have cultivated their unyielding
    detachment.
Betrayal—several of them fallen overnight, without
    warning.
Should I chop you up to draw out your scarce juice,
Or let you rot?
Or should I gather just the scent of your decay?
To mature is to become a dull, blind spot.
Those stones, still unable to fall, tremble

Toward the air-blue sky where crows fly.
Wind, I deserve your lashing.
Desire, when could I ever be a quince for you?

고요의 바다

모퉁이 통창에 반사되는 전자 광고판의 점멸
달의 저편으로 날아가는 모스 부호

긴 머리 그림자가 등장하자
나는 키 작은 그림자로 그 옆에 선다
먼 밖에서 가까운 안에 영사되는 흑백
무대는 창가 천장으로 기울어가는
마름모꼴 캔버스이지만
그림자는 피아노 곁에 기대섰다가
아까부터 양탄자 연속무늬에 드러누워
난 널 다 알고 있다는 듯
느릿하게 고개를 흔든다
어두운 빛 혹은 희미한 어둠으로
아주 환하지 않게 너무 깜깜하지 않게
밖이 안으로 그러다 안이 밖으로 저절로 꺾이는
길거리 춤꾼으로
허공의 비상구 자물쇠통을 여는 마임 연기자로
이렇게 우리는 여름밤을 난다
불면이 연출하는 환희에서 비탄까지
그림자극에선 다들
바다로 가는 기차를 탄다
모래밭에서 구르다 젖다 반짝인다
커튼콜에 연이어 허리를 접는 파도, 파도
밤의 열기가 부드럽게 가라앉고 있다

고요의 바다에서 찬 우유를 꺼낸다
귀 밝은 토끼가 제 발등을 돌도끼로 찍는다

The Sea of Tranquility

The flickering of an electronic billboard reflects in the
    corner of the window,
Morse code messages flying to the far side of the moon.

A long-haired shadow appears,
I stand beside it, a shorter one.
The stage tilts toward the ceiling near the window,
Projected in black and white, from the distant outside to
    the close inside.
Walking out of the rhombus-shaped canvas overhead,
The shadow leans for a moment against the piano,
Then lies down on the continuous pattern of the carpet,
Nodding slowly, as if to say, I know you all.
As street dancers turn their outsides in, their insides out,
As mime performers unlock invisible exits in midair,
In a light that's neither too bright nor too dark,
This is how we spend our summer nights.
Everything in the shadow play, produced by insomnia,
From joy to grief, rides a train to the sea,
Rolling over silver sands, getting wet, sparkling on and
    on—
Waves bowing over and over at the curtain call. Waves,
    waves.
The heat of the night is gently subsiding.

I take out cold milk from the Sea of Tranquility;
The rabbit with sharp ears stabs her own foot with a
  stone ax.

다섯 시 반의 덫은 나의 닻

가장 구석진 곳에
흔적 없이 웅크리고 싶은 시간
곤두선 고양이를 엄호하듯
세상의 모든 실루엣이 나를 감싸고
스치는 빛과
스미는 어둠의 대치에서
골목이 비좁게 탄다
고맙다, 그렇게 살아 있구나
불에 씻긴 불이 숨에 숨긴 숨을
오직 이글거리는 눈빛으로 맑게 내쉬는
딱 그 정점의 제련에서
둥글게 피는 홍반
왜 불타는 얼음장처럼
서늘하게 녹는지
볼수록 가려지는지 헤아리지 못한다
용암구가 열리고 있다
다섯 시 반의 귀로
겨울이 두 발로 서 있다
당신이 보내는 연기 신호를 기다리고 있다
골목에 깔리는 어둠의 무쇠 덫
초공간의 문을 슬쩍 열어주는 석양의 닻
두 족쇄에 묶여 있다

The 5:30 Trap Is My Anchor

This moment, I long to crouch,
And disappear unnoticed into the most secluded place.
All the silhouettes surround me,
As if to shield a bristling cat
Between the passing light and the seeping darkness.
The alley burns in a narrow standoff.
Thank you—for being alive, over there.
A round rash blooms
At the precise peak of smelting,
Fire bathed in fire, breath hidden in breath,
Released only through a gaze ablaze.
Why is it, like burning ice, that it coolly melts?
The more I see, the more it conceals—
It eludes my understanding.
The lava crater opens.
At 5:30's return,
Winter stands on two feet,
Awaiting the smoke signal you send.
The iron-dark trap set in the alley,
And the anchor of the sunset,
Gently prying open the door to hyperspace—
I am bound between two shackles.

쓸쓸

지금 당신은
그네에 걸터앉은 싸락눈의 흔들
시소의 저쪽 너머에서 지긋이 나를 내려다보는
동간 하늘의 눈살
그러니까 당신은 텅 빈 놀이터를 덧껴입고 있다
까치 서넛 맴돌고 있는 배후가
당신의 조끼 단추를 남김없이 채웠다
이름 모를 새는 날아갔다
수만 장의 은행잎이 물들고 졌다
눈밭의 검은 윤기
야밤의 하얀 광택
지금 당신은
손길 혹은 눈길이 만물에 일으키는
상련(相憐)의 소음이다
가지 않은 길이 일으키는 현기증
가까워질수록 확실해지는 종착역의 부재
어제 끈 향초에 오늘 불을 붙이면
심지가 그을음과 함께 탄다
지금 당신은
요가 수련생처럼
다리 하나의 나무 자세로 서있다
명상은 소음에서 시작한다
곧 고양이를 거쳐 코브라가 될 것이다
잔뜩 껴입은 강아지가 풀린 끈을 끌면서

시선이 닿지 않는 미끄럼틀 밑까지
발자국을 찍고 있다
그걸 따라 뛰고 있는 마음의 율동
그러니까 지금 우리의 쓸쓸은
각자의 표정이 아니라
세상 모든 것의 허파에 잠입하여
세상 모든 것의 핏줄기를 타고 흘러가는
아예 어디든 얹혀살고 있는
기생오라비 심보

Lonely

Now, you are the swaying
Of snow pellets, perched on the swing,
And the frown of the winter sky, gently looking down
At you from the other side of the seesaw.
You wear the empty playground around you,
While a few magpies, circling behind, have fastened
All the buttons on your vest.
A nameless bird has flown away,
And thousands of ginkgo leaves have yellowed and
    fallen.
The black sheen of the snowfield,
The white gloss of the night.
Now, you are the noises
Stirred by your compassion
For whatever you touch or glance at.
The dizziness from paths not taken.
The nearer you get, the more certain
The absence of a final stop becomes.
Light yesterday's extinguished candle today,
And the wick burns with soot.
Now, you are standing in tree pose,
Balanced on one leg like a yoga practitioner.
Meditation begins with noise.
Soon, your posture will change from a cat to a cobra.

A heavily dressed puppy, dragging its loose leash,
Leaves footprints beneath the unreachable slide.
Your heart pulses to its rhythm.
So, loneliness now
Is not just an individual complexion,
But the twisted mind of a parasitic brother,
Infiltrating the lungs of everything,
Flowing through the veins of all things,
Feeding off life everywhere.

흰눈깨비 날리는 저녁의 자태

1.

식후 테이크아웃 커피 향에

시선이 슬쩍 외딴 골목으로 빠져드는

길 밖의 길에서

건네고 싶은 안부가 있다

나를 끌어내린 것은 바로 나

날아가는 것은 뭐든 날아가게 두라

2.

터널을 빠져나와
탁 트인 산간 허공이 투사하는
갓 지은 백치 미소에
브레이크 페달을 밟았으나
쿵, 진눈깨비가 산산이 뿌려졌다

3.

봄날의 진눈깨비는
어찌 지면에 인쇄될 수 있을까

누군가 무릎 꿇은 자세로 마룻바닥을 닦고 있다
땅바닥에 눕지 못하는 어스름

4.

진눈깨비 사이로
흰눈깨비 날리는 저녁 무렵
돌개바람이 용 머리 말아 올린다
뒤엉켜 춤추는 지난해 낙엽을 보아라
공중에서 몸을 섞는
저 손짓 발짓 눈짓에
골반이 열린다
낭중(囊中)이 뛴다
지병이 도질 듯, 그래서 좋다
그냥 이대로 흙바람 품에 안겼다가
봄날 찾아온 눈깨비의 넋을 만난다면
언제나 당신의 부름이겠지
오늘도 당신의 등 너머 쪽으로
우리의 등을 껴안는
허공이겠지

The Figure of an Evening When White Hobgoblin Sleet Drifts Down

1.

When my gaze sneaks into a secluded alley,

In the lingering scent of post-meal takeout coffee,

I long to extend a greeting

On the path beyond the path.

What pulled me down was none other than myself.

Let whatever flies, fly.

2.

At an idiot-white smile,
The mountain's open air freshly projected,
Immediately after escaping a long tunnel,
I pressed the brake pedal to the floor—
Yet, thud—
Only shattering like sleet.

3.

How can they imprint spring sleet upon the ground?

Someone scrubs the floor, down on her knees,
While twilight still cannot rest upon the earth.

4.

On a spring evening,
When white hobgoblin sleet drifts down,
Amid fleeting, mischievous flakes,
A whirlwind curls up a dragon's head.
Look at last year's leaves, tangled in a wild dance,
Their bodies swirling in the air.
Listen to their babbling, with eyes blinking,
Feet stomping, hands snapping.
The pelvic girdle swirls open,
And what's in the pocket begins to pulse.
It feels as though one of my chronic ailments will flare
    up—
And that's fine, even better.
If only I could scatter like dust in the wind,
And let spring's ghost summon me at an ungodly hour.
It will always be your call,
And today, like every day, it's the air
That cradles our backs,
Beyond your shoulders.

요즘

1.

소리가 큰 곳에 산다
그래서일 거다, 달은 소리가 작은 곳에 뜬다
사람이 많은 곳에 산다
그래서일까, 당신이 보이지 않는다

걷다가 멈추는 때
시작은 모호했으나 끝은 비교적 명료해지는 지루한 중간에서
공원 풀밭에 착륙하는 새 떼, 그때

저렇듯 두 날개를 곧게 펴고 석양빛의 기울기로 사뿐 내려앉는
우리의 착지는 여기쯤이면 좋으리라

2.

석제 연단이 둘 엇갈려 있더이다

이쪽 단에 오르니 미시간 호가 압권이고
저쪽 단에 오르니 시카고 시가 휘황하여라

연사도 청중도 떠난 황량한 풀밭인지라
난 멋대로 황제이고 선동가이며 음유시인이겠으나
역시 호기심 많은 과객쯤이리라

이쪽에 서니
누구를 대하여 무엇을 말할 수 있을까
궁리가 시작되기도 전에
잠깐, 아무 말도 하지 마
늪지대를 향하여 개굴거리는 유월의 파충류가 되지 마

저쪽에 서니
연단에 놓였을 밤샘 노트
지움, 밑줄, 반복, 휴지, 흘려 쓴 강조까지
군중에 에워싸여
통째로 몰아가는 호흡을
살려내고 싶더이다

팻말은 없는데
혹시 야외 조각품은 아닌지
방치의 연단에 익명의 논객이 등단하였더이다

누구의 것도 아니리라
작자는 의도의 오류를 낳을 것이오
독자는 감정의 오류에 빠질 것이니
그대는, 거기 그렇게 그냥 그뿐일 것이리라

3.

엇갈린
두 방향의 자세
보이는 것이 전부여서
보이는 것은 전부가 아니다
내가 보는 것을 너는 못 보고
네가 보는 것을 나는 못 본다
두 연단에 동시에 내려앉는 겨울 햇살
부재를 마주하여 서 있는
민주주의여,
그대는, 요즘 이 모양 이 꼴일 것인가
시카고 미술관 남쪽
산책길의 주인은 링컨 대통령의 좌상
그가 측선에서 심판을 보는 정원에
연단이 둘 맞장 뜨고 있다
맞장구는 없다
환호성도 야유도 없다
너는 도심의 불빛에게
나는 호수의 물빛에게
어깨 나란히 반대로 서 있으니

4.

캐나다 거위 떼가
뉘엿뉘엿 지고 있다

잔디 틈새에 새똥이 말라간다
타다가 꺼진 채
거꾸로 서 있는 담뱃재들
새가 앉았다 떠난 자리에서 풀이 자란다
한껏 뜨거운 속은
광장에 외상을 남긴다
뒤뚱거리는 막귀 청중들
철새가 텃새 되어 엉덩이가 무거워져 가는
저 날개 족속들

5.

광화문 광장에
동상, 플래카드, 스피커, 시멘트, 차벽, 다 걷어낸 터에
새똥이 말라 부스러져가는 풀밭을 일구고
거기 딱 두 개
맞장 연단이 세워진다면
서로 엇갈려 앞은 탁 트이게
보이는 것을
보이는 대로
실컷,
어긋맞게 딴짓을 할 수 있다면
어긋맞게 딴말을 할 수 있다면

These Days

1.

I live in a cacophonous place.
Perhaps that's why the moon rises in quieter spaces.
I live where there are many people—
Is that why I can't see you?

One day, I will stop walking in the tedious middle,
When, despite the vague beginning, the end becomes
    relatively clear,
And a flock of birds lands on the park grass—at that
    very moment.

I hope our landing can be here,
Spreading two wings horizontally, descending softly in
    the light of the setting sun.
Here, around here, would be a good place for our
    landing.

2.

Two stone platforms were set against each other.

Stepping onto this platform, you would see Lake
    Michigan, breathtaking.

On that platform, the city of Chicago, dazzling.

In the desolate grassland,
Where both the speaker and the audience had departed,
I could suit myself as an emperor, agitator, or minstrel—
But, as you expected, I would be just a curious traveler.

Once I stood on one side,
I could almost hear a voice say:
Wait, don't speak.
Don't become a June reptile croaking toward the
    swamp,
Not even knowing what to say, or to whom.

Yet, standing on the other side,
Surrounded by the crowd,
I almost wished to revive the speaker's breath and
    gestures—
Gathering everything—the overnight notes placed on
    the podium—
Erasing, underlining, repeating, pausing,
And hastily scribbled emphases.

Casting myself as an anonymous critic,
On platforms of neglect, unmarked by any plaque,

I wonder if they should become an outdoor sculpture.

It would belong to no one.
The author would introduce intentional errors;
The reader would fall into emotional ones.
So you, there, will simply be as you are—
Nothing more, nothing less.

3.

Two stances,
In opposite directions.
Seeing is everything,
So what is seen is not everything.
What I see, you cannot.
What you see, I cannot.

The winter sunlight descends
Simultaneously on two platforms
Facing absence.
O democracy,
Is this what you've become these days?
In the promenade south of the Chicago Art Institute,
Where Lincoln's seated statue is the only owner,
In the garden where he watches from the sideline as a

lonely judge,
There are two platforms set against each other—
No back-channel utterances,
No cheers, no boos.
You for the city lights,
I for the lake's reflection,
Parallel yet positioned inversely, shoulder to shoulder.

4.

A flock of Canadian geese was landing with the dusk,
Bird droppings drying between the grass,
Like burnt-out cigarette ashes still standing upright.
Grass grows where the birds have landed and gone.

Whatever burns intensely to the core
Leaves scars in the square where migratory
Birds become sedentary, their hips growing heavier—
That stumbling, tone-deaf audience.

5.

If only we could clear Gwanghwamun Square
Of statues, placards, speakers, cement, and vehicle
    barriers,

And let grass grow where bird droppings dry and
    crumble.
If only two opposing platforms were set up there,
Intersecting each other,
With their fronts always open—
To see what is seen, just as it is,
As much as we wish.
So we can act in our own ways,
So we can speak in our own pleasures.

반(半)-내림

광활한 너울이 모래 언덕 쪽으로 둥글게 넘어가는 저녁의 통(桶) 속에 있어요

먼 데서 밀려온 요동이 바람 그친 이승에 긴 파랑(波浪)을 일으키는군요

공소시효가 소급되는 현장에는 혼자라는 미제사건이 스멀거리지요

요즘은 종종 남성에서 중성으로 키가 바뀌고 플랫 되는 음이 발생해요

청색 소음이 분광(分光)에 일으키는 착란, 세상이 둘에서 셋으로 갈라지다가 분말로 번지기도 하지요

비 오는 날의 김 서린 차창 밖이거나 세 번 깨었다 네 번 잠이든 혼몽 속일 거예요

응시, 소용돌이치는 먼 흑점이 까마귀 그림자에서 꺼져가는 숯으로 그러다 한 획 먹물로 말라가요

아버지를 태운 완행버스는 읍내로 멀어지고 뒤에 남은 아이가 홀로 마을로 돌아갈 궁리를 했어요

신작로가 서서히 좁아져 소실점으로 사라지는 사방에서 광대한 저녁이 무채색으로 압착 되었어요

어스름은 뒤에 남겨진 자의 숨결이라는 걸 예감하게 되었죠, 어스름의 살갗에 살며시 파고든 손톱, 그 아린 감촉, 어떤 촉은 한곳에 오래 머물다가 아예 눌러살기도 하지요

이렇게 세상이 잔잔히 가라앉는 땅끝이면 쓸쓸함조차 꽤 단맛이 나요

내가 잡을 수는 없으나 나를 붙잡고 있는 것에게는 척, 악수를 청

하는 게 상책이겠지요

그것이 나를 바닷가에 끌어내고 종소리를 듣게 하고 당신의 시를 필사하게 했지요

가깝게 다가섰다고 여겼어요, 앞에서 간혹 대할 때보다 뒤에서 불현듯 안아줄 때 까마득히 가까운 운명이라고 느꼈어요

아득한 불안과 이유 없는 그리움이 수시로 자리 깔고 누웠지요

아무도 가르쳐주지 않았으나 당신을 가장 깊은 곳에 심었어요

아무도 알려주지 않아서 혼자의 음계를 조율했지요

반(半)-내림, 고독이라는 단어를 알기 전부터 몸이 감내해온 것이 써내는 조표(調標)

물정에 길들기 전에 나를 압도했던 것의 흑백 인화

이제 물에 씻긴 자갈처럼 말갛게 그 자리에 박혀 있을 뿐

이렇게 기억의 어스름과 공명을 이루는 날이면

그 둥글게 넘어가는 너울의 낯바닥을 미끄러져 당신 가까이 흰 거품으로 부서지면

다음 날 들녘 가득 아침 안개가 피어요

당신이 어쩌다 실수로 선사한 서너 줄 시구가 떠올라요

그 은은한 반올림의 영성으로 심장을 씻으려는데 난 여전히 온몸이 가렵고

오늘 당신은 (따라서 나도) 다시 반-내림 중이에요

In a Half-Flat Key

I'm in the vast barrel of evening, which swells and rolls
   toward the sand dunes.
A distant stir from afar raises long waves in the windless
   world.
In this scene, where the statute of limitations is
   retroactive,
The cold cases of being alone creep back in.
These days, the key often shifts from masculine to
   neutral, and flat notes appear.
The confusion caused by blue noise splits the spectrum,
Dividing the world from two into three, sometimes
   scattering it into powder.
It's like the mist on a car window during a rainy day,
Or the blurry state between waking three times and
   sleeping four.
I gaze—watching as a distant black spot in a whirlpool
   fades
From the shadow of a crow to charcoal, drying into a
   single stroke of ink.
The slow bus to downtown, carrying my father, recedes
Between poplar trees where the road curves into dust.
The child left behind ponders returning home alone.
As the bumpy, pebbled pavement narrows and
   disappears into a vanishing point,

The vast hollow of evening compresses into
monochrome.
I had a strange feeling that twilight is the breath of
those left behind,
Its ethereal layer of dusk like skin,
Where my fingernails often softly dig, stirring a tender,
aching touch—
Some touches linger and remain under the skin
indefinitely.
At the world's quiet end, even loneliness has a sweet
flavor.
When I cannot grasp it, it's best to shake hands with
what holds me.
It led me to the seashore, made me hear the bells,
And transcribe your poetry.
I thought I had come closer, more intimate,
Feeling the proximity of distant fate—
More so when embraced from behind than when
occasionally facing you.
Vague anxieties and inexplicable longing often settle
within me.
No one taught me, but I knew how to plant you deep
inside me.
No one acknowledged me, so I tuned my own scale.

Half-flat, the signature key my body endured
Before I learned the word loneliness.
The black-and-white impressions of what overwhelmed
　　me
Before I became accustomed to the world.
Now, I remain embedded in place, unmoving, like
　　pebbles washed by the water.
Whenever I resonate with the dusk of memory,
Every time I glide across the hollow crest of the
　　rounding swell,
Breaking into white foam near you,
The next day, the fields are veiled in morning mist.
A few lines of verse, accidentally gifted by you, come to
　　mind,
And I try to wash my heart with their subtle spirituality
　　in a half-sharp key.
Yet my whole body still itches,
And today, you (and therefore I) are in a half-flat key
　　once again.

찻물 식어가는 소리

내가 좋아하는 유리잔은
생수를 부으면 아기 눈을 초롱초롱 뜨지
적포도주를 담아 가벼이 돌릴 때는
올리브 빛 하늘이 연하게 탄화하기도 하지
내 빈틈을 상냥하게 파고드는 도시의 사냥꾼
적막에 냉큼 끼어들어 반갑다 손을 잡아끄는
잘생긴 유리 찻잔
늘 곁을 지키지
차가 우러나는 시간
우리는 어찌 우러나는 것일까
오늘은 저 투명한 잔을 쥐고
싹 치운 후 아직 아무것도 펼쳐지지 않은
아침 마당으로 가야지
내 유리잔에는 무엇이든 풀어지고 있지
히비스커스, 남몰래 간직한 사랑의 신맛
녹차, 찻잎이 녹여낸 언덕 햇살은 밝은 노랑
끓고 휘돌고 우러나고 가라앉고
밋밋하게 식어가는 찻물에
세상 잡맛이 심심하게 누그러지고 있어
안부라도 묻듯
시간에 묶인 시간을 풀어내듯
가득 찬 잔을 들고 손톱 끝으로 쳐 봐
볼멘소리가 돌아오지
이제 거의 바닥이 드러나는 즈음

저걸 검지로 튕기면 어떤 소리가 날까
빈 잔의 소리는 청아하겠지
해도, 당신의 빈 잔과 부딪는 일은 삼가야겠어
때늦은 공명은 감내하기 어려울 테니

The Sound of Tea Cooling

The glass I love sparkles
Like a baby's eyes when filled with fresh water.
When I swirl red wine lightly inside it,
A faint olive sky sometimes smokes softly.
Like a city hunter, gently intruding into my silent
    crevices,
Cheerfully grasping my hand,
This handsome tea glass
Always stays by my side.
As the tea leaves soak in hot water,
How do we steep ourselves?
Today, holding that transparent glass,
I'll step into the morning yard,
Where nothing has yet unfolded after its tidy-up.
In my glass, anything can dissolve—
Hibiscus, the secret sourness of hidden love,
Green tea, the bright yellow of hillside sunlight
Extracted from early-May leaves.
In the tea water, cooling blandly
After boiling, swirling, steeping, and settling,
The world's mixed flavors plainly mellow out.
As if to inquire after each other's well-being,
To untangle time bound by time,
I tap the full glass with my fingertip,

And a soft grumble returns.

Now, with the bottom almost revealed,

What sound will it make if I flick it with my index
finger?

The sound of an empty glass must be clear.

Yet I must refrain from clinking it against your empty
glass,

For our delayed resonance might be too much to bear.

4
그늘 한 칸의 골상학

마음이 내쉬는 선의 속성.
내가 나를 본다. 나는 넓어지는 각도이다,
그런데도 이러한 실행은 급속도로—
각 지점에 그리고 다음의 올바른 지점에 못을 치고,
서로 잠그면서, 교정하고, 다시 교정하여, 각각의 올바름
이 찰깍 헐거워지더니
떠다니다가, 허공에 걸렸다가, 소용돌이치다가, 드디어
씨앗-내림,
재빠르다—이제부터는 가시적인 것의 증거가—이제부터
는, 헐거워짐이—

　　—조리 그레이엄, 〈자아의 실체에 관한 비망록〉,
　　　　《통합장의 꿈》, 160.

IV
Phrenology of a Shaded Haven

The nature of goodness the mind exhales.
I see myself. I am a widening angle of
and nevertheless and this performance has rapidly—
nailing each point and then each next right point,
   inter-locking, correct, correct again, each
   rightness snapping loose,
floating, hook in the air, swirling, seed-down,
quick—the evidence of the visual henceforth—and
   henceforth, loosening—

   —Jorie Graham, "Notes on the Reality of the Self,"
     The Dream of the Unified Field, 160.

오월이 오면

메에, 운다
풀을 뜯다가 고갤 든 염소는
두 눈이 검게 빛나서
지금만 같아라, 그쯤 뜻하는 듯해서
나도 메에, 녹울대를 흔들어 본다
메에, 운다고 다 서글픈 것은 아닌데
그립다고 다 목젖이 뜨거워지는 것은 아닌데
한 손으로 저녁 햇살을 가렸다가
손가락 사이로 흘려보내는데
데가 끊기지 않아서
생은 이어져 가는 것인데
세상의 뇌관을 제거하는 오월의 아카시아 향
먼저 떠난 이들이
그윽한 시절을 데리고 차창에 어른거리는 덜컹거림에서
부르지 않아도 찾아와
외면하게 되는 것이 있듯
유리에 비치는 유령의 시간은
타협을 말하고 불순을 말하고 미완성을 말하고
해도, 그런 것 이제 와 덧없이 여겨지고
오늘의 메뉴가 궁금해지고
아무리 달래도 아이는 울고
시선에 아랑곳하지 않는 입술이 부딪고
수화기에 대고 연신 사장님을 찾고
고에서 고로 끝없이 이어져

기차는 전진한다
역방향은 꼬리에 달거나
간혹 머리에 이고 달린다
부른다고 모두가 응하지는 않으나
그런 줄 알면서도 부르게 되는 것들
두 뿔을 잡고 씨름했던 염소
광주의 길거리마다 목마름으로 외쳤던 그녀의 가두방송
오월이 오면
환승역 지나 먼발치에 희끗희끗
아카시아꽃이 연달아 손짓하면

When May Comes

"Baa," it bleats.
The goat pauses its grazing,
Lifting its head, eyes dark and shining,
As if to say, "May this moment never end."
I, too, cry, "baa," shaking my throat.
Not every cry is sorrowful.
Not every longing sears the throat.
Not every hand blinds the eyes.
Even if fingers block the evening light,
Life endures, as long as "though" persists.
The scent of May's acacia disarms the world's detonator.
Always clattering are the southward windows,
Where those who departed first glimmer,
Entwined with old times.
At times, we flinch from what knocks, even unbidden.
The ghostly hours waver in the glass,
Reflecting faint echoes of compromise, impurity,
    incompletion.
Yet these things now seem futile.
We are simply curious about today's menu.
The baby cries, no matter how her mother soothes her.
Lips clash, indifferent to the neighbor's gaze.
The man keeps reporting to his boss over the phone.
Endlessly passed on—one to another, whatever it is—

The train moves forward,

Its reverse-direction locomotive trailing behind

Or sometimes leading from the front.

Not everything answers when called,

Yet some things return unbidden—

The goat I wrestled with, its horns and dark eyes,

The thirsty shouts she broadcast across Kwangju streets.

When May comes,

And white acacia blossoms loom beyond the halfway
    station,

Beckoning in the distance, one after another.

아주 오래된 오늘

숨이 멎는 순간에 시작되는
항상 그 자리에 있는 오늘
정거장을 덮치는 아파트
버스 뒷자리에 압사하는 귀가
뉘우치지 않는 자의 육신이
묻힐 곳을 찾지 못한다
어제로 멀어지지 않아
내일이 다가오지 않는 오늘
바람에 흔들리는 대교
날개 없이 추락하는 안전모
시퍼런 물속에서 보내온 마지막 문자
오늘이 켜켜이 쌓인다
눈먼 돌개바람에 휩쓸려
미친 듯 뒤집히는 청보리라면
산산이 부서지는 낭떠러지 파도라면
저편 어딘들 넘어갈 수 있으련만

A Very Old Today

Today, steadfast in its place, begins
At the moment breath ceases.
The bus stop devoured by a crumbled apartment,
The journey home, crushed in the bus's rear seat.
A once-powerful body, unyielding,
Finds no place to rest.
Tomorrow holds back,
For today refuses to dissolve into yesterday.
A bridge sways in the wind,
A helmet plummets, wingless,
The final message sent from the cold, blue depths.
Today piles up, layer upon layer.
If only a blind whirlwind could sweep it away,
If only it were green barley thrashing wildly,
Or waves shattering against a sheer cliff—
Then, perhaps, we could cross to the other side.

그라운드 제로

밑줄과 마주 선다
하늘 아래 반듯이 누운 당신의 골격을 읽는다
한 발이 헛디디면 잽싸게
다른 발을 내딛는 나
깨금발로 서서 더 멀리 보려는 나
마냥 서 있으려는 나
기껏해야 순간의 중심을 견디는 나를 향해
박동을 멈춘 당신
풀밭의 심전도에, 그라운드 제로에 직선을 새긴다
길게 널브러진 십 리 들길에서
난 어찌 직립보행일까?

Ground Zero

Facing the vast expanse,
I trace the underline of you,
Lying straight beneath the sky.
When one foot falters,
I shift quickly to the other.
I rise on tiptoe, straining to see farther,
Standing as best I can, as needed,
Holding steady in the heart of the moment.
But you—a pulse gone still—
Imprint a flat line
Across the grass's electrocardiogram,
At ground zero.
Along a six-mile stretch of sprawling fields,
How do I still walk upright?

빗길에 운전 중

수천 잎이 출렁이는
넝쿨의 키를 누가 잴 수 있을까
휘고 숨은 굽이는 어찌 계산하고
담장을 넘어간 자유의지는 어찌 셈할까
동서를 잇는 방음벽을 휘덮고서
남북을 푸르게 넘나들고 있다
흰 밥알을 배급하는 조팝나무
화정동 고개 사건을 주렁주렁 고발하는
수십 그루 아카시아꽃의 흰 함성
나루터 갯버들이 부들부들 털을 곤두세우자
빗길에서 누군가, 꽝
앞서가는 차의 꽁무니를 받는다
멀어지는 자의 항적에서 부옇게 일어나
따라가는 자의 창에 뿌려지는 분무
집어삼키면서 뱉어내면서
수직으로 올랐다가 수평으로 기었다가
수천 잎이 일으키는 너울성 물결이
도도하게 흘러가고 있다
강변도로 넝쿨을 따라 서행 중
빗길에 운전 중

Driving in the Rain

Who can measure the height of the vine,
As thousands of leaves ripple in unison?
How could one calculate the hidden bends,
Or the free spirit that stretches beyond the fence?
Covering the tall sound barriers that bridge east to west,
It roams freely, painting everything green
As it crosses north and south.
The deutzia tree scatters white grains like rice balls,
And the white clamor of acacia clusters hangs heavily,
Laden with stories of the Hwajung Hill mishaps.
As willows by the ferry quiver, bristling their fur,
Someone on the rainy road—bang—
Crashes into the car ahead.
A spray from the trail of the one going before
Spatters across the window of the one following.
As the vine engulfs and spits out,
Rising upright, stretching sideways,
The billowing waves stirred by thousands of leaves
Flow with a dignified grace.
Creeping along the riverside road,
Winding along vine after vine,
I drive cautiously in the rain.

카운트다운

비 갠 후
서울의 낮빛이 돌아왔다
모두 제자리여서 반갑다
거리가 붐비기 시작하는 점심시간
한 끼의 수다를 찾아
오늘도 기꺼이 떠날 것이다
재스민향을 따라 얼룩말 띠무늬를 밟자
서른에서 카운트다운이 시작된다
거꾸로 가는 시간은
항상 제로에서 안색을 바꾼다
모퉁이 은행에서 우회전이 불안
보도블록의 연속무늬를 조심하라
그곳이 그곳인 곳에
무너지는 빈칸이 있다
이음매 속에 숨어 사는 모서리
갈라서자 바로 날을 세우는 각도가 있다
정장에 인식표를 드리우고
세상의 요철을 따라가는 정오의 리듬
누군가 기울면 누군가 기울고
아무나 서면 아무나 서고
도미노가 도착하는 끝에
유리문이 닫히고 있다
수년을 다니던 든든한 길이지만
오늘 술렁이고 있다

빗물이 할퀴고 지나간 어젯밤
발길 아래 물길이 얼마나 헤집었는지
딛자마자 꺼지는 여기저기
빈속에서 누런 위액이 솟는다
구수한 순두부를 찾아가는
길 아래 길이
수상하다

Countdown

After the rain clears,
Seoul's familiar face returns,
And everything falls back in place.
At lunchtime, the streets start to bustle,
Each step in search of conversation over a meal.
Today, too, I set off gladly,
Following jasmine's scent, stepping on zebra stripes.
The countdown starts at thirty,
Time running backward,
Its face always changing at zero.
A right turn at the corner bank brings unease—
Watch for the sidewalk's endless patterns.
A blank space collapses—
In a place like any other.
Corners live, hidden in seams;
Parted, angles form instantly, sharply.
Dropping its ID tag over the suit,
Midday rhythm follows the world's uneven road.
When one tilts, another tilts;
When one stands, another stands.
At the end of the dominoes' path,
A glass door closes.
A steady path I've walked for years—
Today, though, it feels uneasy.

Clawed through by last night's rain,
How much was unearthed beneath my feet?
Sinking here and there, each step I take—
From an empty stomach, yellow bile rises.
On the way to savory tofu stew,
The road beneath the road
Feels suspicious.

라르고

꽃이 진 자리
마른 화분이 지키고 있다
남겨진 것들의 뜨락에
물 조리개를 들고 서성이는 저녁
무성음이 발음하기 어려운 것은
모음이 안아주지 않아서이건만
산에 답이 있다는
먼저 먼 길 떠난 선배의 말은
아마 답이 없다는 촉(觸)이었을 듯
믿기지 않을수록 믿으려 우기는
자발적 맹신의 역설법이었을 수도
지금쯤 그늘진 산길은
겉만 녹아서 질척이겠지
스며들지 못하고 마르지 않아
어쩌면 다시 봄눈이 쌓였을지도
등산화를 떡칠하고 바지 밑단까지 들러붙는
겨울 잔해에서 봄소식까지
그냥 그대로 끈적이는 대로
무방비가 최선일 듯
방구석에 이르는 유일한 길은 골목일 수도
기립한 건물 실루엣 사이에서
입구인 듯 출구인 듯 불콰하게
술기운이 올랐다가 식어가는 석양은
지상에 앉은 더께의 시간을
어찌 저리 발갛게 사를까?

Largo

Dry pots stand sentinel
Where the flowers have fallen.
Evening wanders with a watering can
Through the yard of what remains.
Voiceless consonants are hard to pronounce,
Because vowels refuse to embrace them.
When an elder who departed earlier once said,
"The answer is in the mountain,"
It seems he was only hinting
That there is no answer.
The more unbelievable, the more one insists—
A paradox of willing blind faith.
By now, the shaded mountain paths
Are probably softening, surface melting into mud,
Unable to seep in, not yet dry.
Perhaps spring snow has piled up once more.
Just leave it sticky, as it is,
From winter's remnants, caking boots
And clinging to pant cuffs,
To the looming hint of spring.
Perhaps defenselessness is the wiser strategy.
The only path to the room's corner may be an alley.
Between upright silhouettes of buildings,
The sunset flushes, an entrance, an exit—
How does it burn time's layers upon the earth

Into so crimson?

후후

한 다발 수국이
침상까지 따라왔다
한강 야경에 소문 없이
꽂혀 있던 서너 송이 꽃
주메뉴가 끝나자 수거되었다가
셔터가 터지고 함성이 솟고
다른 서너 송이와 다시 묶여
손에 쥐어졌다
60층에서 지하 4층으로
B30 기둥을 돌아 지상으로
흩어지는 낯선 차들을 따라
아무도 막지 않는 유려한 흐름 속으로
시간이 미끄러졌다
쉰내가 풍기는 단지에는
간혹 주정 꽃이 피는 게 있다
잠 못 들던 때가 그립지는 않으나
헤어지고 사라져도 그다지 아프지는 않으나
당기는 대로 풀리는 매듭
우다방 계단에 앉아
돌아오지 않는 강을 부른다
예식장 샹들리에 아래에서
두꺼운 스테이크를 썰었는데
골목 식당 백열전구 불빛에 싸여
끓는 라면을 사이에 두고

이별을 선고받으면서
후후, 벌써 시들해진 한 다발 수국에
입김을 불고 있다

Hoo-Hoo

A bunch of hydrangeas
Followed me to my bedside.
As the shutter clicked and cheers erupted,
Three or four blooms,
Silently lodged in the Han River nightscape,
Were cleared away after the main course,
Then rejoined others,
Clasped in my hand.
Time slipped into the graceful flow,
Rounding column B30,
From floor 60 to basement level 4,
Unfamiliar cars dispersing above ground,
With no one to stop them.
In a pot sour with age,
Sometimes an alcoholic flower appears.
I no longer long for sleepless nights,
Nor do separation and loss sting as deeply as before.
Knots untangle as easily as they tighten—
A boy hums "The River of No Return"
Sitting on the steps of PO Cafe.
After a thick steak
Beneath the wedding hall chandelier,
Now wrapped in the glow of incandescent bulbs
In a back-alley diner,

Parting over a pot of instant noodles,
Hoo-hoo, I breathe onto
The already withered bunch of hydrangeas.

널 목 졸라 죽이고도

지퍼가 없어서
널 여는 유일한 방법은
사정없이 외피를 찢는 것이다
단번에 점령할 재주는 없다
꼭 쥐고서 이리저리 돌려세운다
제발 어서 녹으라고 닦달한다
두세 차례 물어뜯어야
가까스로 드러나는 너의 속
얼음투성이가 입안으로 들어오다가 그친다
속속들이 물러질 때까지
기다릴 짬은 없다
손에 묻은 진액을 핥는다
길 위의 입맛이 이렇듯 정직할 줄이야
깨물고 짜고 빨고
마지막 알갱이까지
탄탄하던 백옥이 쭈그러진 반투명 허물로
여름 하늘에서 곤두박질칠 때까지
짐승의 아가리에 턴다
쭈쭈바,
널 목 졸라 죽이고도
싸구려 단맛에 내 불타는 영혼을 팔고서도
아, 여전히 목이 타는구나

Even After Strangling You to Death

Because there's no zipper,
The only way to open you
Is to rip through your outer layer, mercilessly.
Lacking the skill to conquer you in one go,
I grip you tight, turning you this way and that,
Desperately willing you to melt faster.
A few bites in, your insides barely surface.
Chunks of ice come to a standstill in my mouth—
I don't have time to wait
For you to soften completely.
Sticky juice lingers on my hands as I lick it off.
Who knew a taste on the road could be this honest?
Biting, squeezing, sucking—
To the very last bit,
You're tossed into the beast's maw
Until solid white jade crumples to a translucent husk
And drops from the summer sky.
Squeeze Ice Pop,
Even after wringing out every last drop,
Even after trading my searing soul for that cheap
    sweetness—
Ah, my thirsty throat still burns.

어떤 잠입

들어가고 보는 것이다
막아 세우는 이는 없어도
어쩌려나 싶게 쳐다보는 이가 있겠지만
속으로 쑥 직진하는 것이 첫 수
둘째 수는 그러니까
어차피 아는 게 별로 없으므로
그렇다고 저어하고 눈치 보고 그래서는 촌놈이므로
촌놈 맞으나 굳이 광고할 일은 아니므로
있는 것 없는 것
자신 있게 뜯어보는 것이다
사실, 없는 것 들여다보는 게
내가 속한 직업군의 특기가 아니던가
맛없다 싶으면 단번에 뱉고
그렇다고 바닥에 버릴 일은 노, 노
사는 게 그렇듯 속으로 뱉고
유료 관람자의 느긋한 걸음으로
또 하나의 대상을 향해 나아가는 것이다
마음에 담을 양이면
너무 가까이는 다가가지 말고
차라리 카메라의 확대 기능을 이용하여
예의는 간당간당 지키면서
당기고 밀고 기울이고 젖히고
뭐든 끄집어내는 것이다
혹자는 한자리에서 오래 죽치는 것이

장소를 관통하는 멋진 방식이라고 하지만
세상은 넓고 볼 것은 많으니
해가 짧은 오후
어차피 여기 뿌리내릴 수도
이야기를 예서 끝낼 수도 없으니
비망록은 한 쪽을 넘기지 않으리라
그냥 지나칠 일이다
어쩌다 동쪽에서 들어와서는
아마 남쪽으로 나가도 그만일 것
남겨진 시간을 아름답게 소진한다는 것은
걷다가 서고 걷다가 서는
찰나의 잠입일 것

A Certain Infiltration

It's about entering without a second thought.
Though no one stops you,
Someone might look at you, wondering what you're up
    to.
But the first step is to stride right in.
The second step is, well, to confidently survey what's
    there
And what isn't—since you know little about it anyway.
Showing hesitation or excess caution might
Mark you as a country bumpkin.
You might be one, but why advertise it?
In fact, isn't it a specialty of our profession
To peer into what isn't there?
If it tastes bad, spit it out at once—
But not on the ground.
Just as in life, swallow it inwardly.
And with the unhurried steps of a paying spectator,
Move on to another object.
If it's something you'd want to hold in your heart,
Don't get too close—
Instead, use the zoom function of a camera.
Maintain just enough courtesy:
Pull in, push out, tilt, bend—
Capture whatever you can.

Some say lingering long in one spot
Is a cool way to penetrate a scene.
But the world is vast, and there's much to see,
And the afternoon is short.
Anyway, you can't put down roots here,
Nor can you end the story here.
The memo will not be longer than one page.
Let it just pass by.
If you entered by chance from the east,
You might as well exit to the south.
To spend the remaining time beautifully means
To stop, walk, stop, walk—
A fleeting infiltration.

시카고 문화 센터

아무도 막지 않으니
들어가도 그만 나가도 그만
대리석 홀 한가운데서
계단이 과객을 잡아 올린다
층과 층 사이에 잠시 쉬게 하고
양편 두 갈래로 선회시키더니
천천히 밀어 넣는다
이 방에서 저 방으로
딴 세상으로 가는 통로가 열린다
한눈팔기에 넉넉한 문양과 글귀가
사방에 돋아 있다
층마다 방마다
다른 시간이 전시되겠지만
계단은 늘 저대로 있겠지
그 아래 그늘이 자라고 있다
그 속에 앉아 딴생각 중이다
상승 계단이 넓으니
그렇게 하강 처마도 깊겠지
두 계단이 허공에서 만났다 헤어지는
발자국 자취 아래
계란형 탁자가 하나
그 안쪽에 가죽 소파가 하나
그 양쪽에 엉덩이 자국이 깊은 의자가 둘
그들이 가만가만 사물의 언어를 소곤대는

벽 없는 방
텅 빈 중앙을 등지고 그 소파에 앉아
창에 노을이 비치기를 기다린다
1층 시니어 작품전을 지나
4층 흑인 역사를 기리는 연설을 지나
5층 올라가는 계단 밑에 쉬고 있다
한동안 방해하는 이가 없으니
이로써 묵은 돌계단 지붕 아래 사랑방의
현 소유권을 주장하는 바이다
낮은 조도의 백열등이 곁눈질하는
낯선 자리 낯선 시간
참 그윽한 저녁에

The Chicago Cultural Center

No one stops you,
Whether you enter or leave—it's all the same.
In the marble hall's center,
The stairs lift you,
Offering a brief rest between floors.
Then, gently turning you aside,
Slowly guiding you
From one room to the next,
Opening a passage to another world.
Patterns and inscriptions, rich distractions,
Sprout everywhere.
Every floor, every room
Reveals a different era,
While the stairs remain unchanged.
They cast shadows where I sit, lost in thought.
If the ascending stairs are wide,
Surely the descending eaves are deep, too.
Two stairs, right and left,
Meet and part in midair.
Beneath faint traces of footsteps,
An oval table waits,
And inside, a leather sofa,
With two chairs on either side, their seats well-worn.
In this room without walls, I hear them,

Softly whispering the language of things.
Sitting on the sofa, my back turned to the void,
I wait for the sunset to shine through the window,
Passing the senior art exhibit on the first floor,
And the speech honoring Black history on the fourth.
Now, I rest beneath the stairs
Leading up to the fifth floor.
For a while, no one disturbs me,
So, beneath the old stone stairway roof,
I claim temporary ownership of this small guest room—
On a truly serene evening,
As low-lit incandescent bulbs cast glances
At a stranger, in a strange time, in a strange place.

장화 신은 느림보

창가 오후가 소란하다
신축 건물 2층에 시작된 콘크리트 타설
한 치의 오차도 없이 평등한 지평을 만들어라
지나온 자리,
일꾼들이 수평을 잡고 있다
널판에 무릎을 꿇고 머리를 조아려
뒤로 물러나고 있는 저이들
쏟아붓는 이가 앞서고
써레질하는 이가 뒤따른다
지상의 명령을 수행하는 데는
순서가 있다
버무리고 붓고 써레질한 결이 의연하여도
물렁한 시간을 마감해줄 버퍼 질이 필요하다
장화 신은 느림보
발은 굼떠도 손은 빠르다
시멘트 늪에 빠지기 싫은 자는
목제 스키라도 신어라
발자국은 절대 남기지 마라
공사장 곁으로 경전철이 지나간다
딱 그 높이에 나타났다 사라지는 수평
도심의 유리 건물들이 저리 당당한 것은
층층이 수평이 잡혀서일 거다
수직 속에 수평이 살고 있다
레미콘이 연이어 도착하고

불 꺼진 골목이 근처에 수군대고
해가 지기 시작하는 해발 2층의 허공에서
흔적마저 지우려는 사내들이
가슴을 쓸어내리고 있다

The Slowpokes in Boots

The afternoon buzzes by the window.
They start to pour concrete on the second floor
Of a new building under construction,
To achieve a flawlessly even, immaculate horizon.
Workers level the surface,
Kneeling on planks, retreating backward with bent
    backs.
The laborer pouring leads; the odd-jobber raking flat
    follows.
There's a rhythm in obeying the earth's commands.
Even once the surface is firmly smoothed—
Through mixing, pouring, and raking—
A final buffing is needed
To tie up this loose, lingering time.
The slowpokes in long boots—
Though their feet are sluggish, their hands are swift.
If you don't want to sink in this cement swamp,
Strap on wooden skis, at the very least.
Leave no footprints.
A light rail train passes by the site,
Appearing and disappearing, always at the same height.
The city's glass buildings stand imposingly,
Because each floor is perfectly leveled.
Horizontals live within verticals.

As the sun dips into the second-floor void,
Whispers recede from a nearby unlit alley.
Cement mixer trucks roll in, one after another,
And the slowpokes pat and brush their chests,
As if dusting off the last faintest vestige

소리가 왕이로소이다

속에서 또 그 속에서
소리 없이 소리를 낸다
세상살이 곳곳에
당신과 언제든 불협화음을 이루는
불가청 저음파가 배어있다
속이 위험하지만
그럴수록 더 깊이 파고드는 버릇
매미 떼가 다시 깨어나고 있다
높아지다가 낮아지는 소리
낮아지다가 높아지는 소리
여름 하늘을 길게 끌면서
녹음 사이 어디론가 건너가는
매미 떼 울음의 포물선
다행이다, 저 소리에는 속이 없다
속에서 그 속에서가 아니라
죽 정상 너머까지 치솟거나
죽 최후 이후까지 치닫고 있다
모든 것을 한 번에 소진하는 방식
시작 속에 끝이 없고
끝 속에 시작이 없다
허물을 벗고
죽어라, 현생을 고하는 떼창
뜨거운 여름날은
이렇게 내 탓도 잊고 네 탓도 사라진
그냥 소리가 왕이로소이다

King Is the Sound

Sound without sound,
From within, and from within yet again,
An inaudible, low frequency
Resides in every corner of life,
Always at odds with you.
Though more dangerous within,
You keep the habit of digging deeper.
Cicada swarms awaken once more—
A sound rises, then falls;
A sound falls, then rises.
The parabolic cry of cicada swarms,
Dragging the summer sky in a sweeping arc,
Crosses somewhere within the greenery.
Thankfully, that sound has no core,
Neither from within, nor within itself.
Yet it soars beyond the highest peak
Or rushes forward past the very edge,
As though exhausting everything at once.
At its beginning, no end exists;
At its end, no beginning exists.
When the old skin is shed,
They sing on this side of life, rushing toward death.
On a scorching summer day,
Simply, sound reigns as king,
Where my faults vanish, and yours are forgotten.

어제도 많은 말을 했다

큰 나무 옆에
선다, 기대고 싶다
물길 따라 다시 걷는다
앞서 흘러가는 강물의 도도한 뒤태
뒤 쳐져도 그만이다
꽃이 다가와
잘 지내느냐고
묻지 않는다, 그냥 지나가기는
바람도 마찬가지다, 한때 나도
씩씩한 만큼 예뻤으므로
돌아보지 않는다
아무 말도 필요 없어
꽃이든 나무든 함께 지낸다
특별한 이유 없이
가끔 만나고 간혹 헤어진다
꽃이 꽃으로
피고 지는 동안
사람들 사이에서
어제도 많은 말을 했다
후배에게 주장을 펼쳤고
선배에게 무능을 가장(假裝)했다
꽃은 벌이 들락거려도 신경 쓰지 않는다
저 강물이 내 곁에 나란하여도
더 빠르게 더 멀리 달아난다

나무가 나무로
제 뿌리를 지키는 동안
기대고 싶다, 어딘가

I Again Talked Too Much Yesterday

Standing beside a tall tree,

I feel an urge to lean on it.

But I resume my walk, following the current.

The river flows ahead with dignity.

It's fine if I fall behind.

A flower comes close,

But it doesn't stop to inquire about me.

The wind does the same.

So I don't look back,

For I, too, was once as strong as I was beautiful.

No words are needed.

I'm at ease sharing this moment and space

With either a flower or a tree.

Sometimes we meet, sometimes we part,

Bound by no special relationship.

When flowers simply bloom and wither,

I realize I talked too much again yesterday among
    people—

Insisting on my views to a junior,

While feigning incompetence to a senior.

Flowers don't mind how bees keep busy,

And the river runs, rushing faster and farther.

The tree holds firmly to its roots,

And I wish I had somewhere to lean.

적에게, 2004

당신의 포개진 무릎에서
숨 한 결에 원고 한 매씩 낱낱이 읽혀
책 무덤에 던져졌소
청춘에 모든 것을 걸고
기쁘게 무너질 수 있는 것은
눈 내리는 창가
세 번째 찻물이 식어가는
오직 당신 앞이어서, 하지만
몸짓과 말투마저 당신에게 맞춰온
아름다운 몽유(夢遊)의 시간
그 그림자의 낙원에 숨이 막혀
나 속에 살던 나 아닌 나를
이제, 타인으로 추방하겠소
화분 속에서 배를 갈랐소
거기 사뭇 웃자란 자줏빛 풀꽃이
제풀에 이울기 전에
들판에 바람의 씨를 던지겠소
당신의 깊이에 이를 수 없다면
당신의 잣대로 내 속을 잰다면
더는 이렇게 나를 괴롭히지 않겠소
안에서 움틀 따름인 것에게
홀로 피어날 용기와 자유를
적(敵)이여, 어깨 너머의 시선이여
본디 나는 이승의 찰나를 지나가는

한 톨 갈색 씨앗
하강하는 참새 떼의 날갯짓에
산산이 흩어지겠소
아니, 공허를 향해 훅
지구본 손에 쥐고 불어대는 입김에
흰 갓털 낙하산을 펴고
달빛 차오르는 어디든 날아가겠소
해마다 닥쳐올 서넛 태풍에
흙투성이 깃털 잎이 머쓱하게 자라는
어쩌면, 앉은뱅이 풀꽃으로 살겠소
그리하여 나 밖에 있는 당신
당신 밖에 있는 또 다른 당신에게
낮은 자세로 가까이 귀동냥할 수 있기를
용서하시오, 벌써 그리운 적이여
이렇게 내가 너무 쉽게 나를
사랑하는 만용을

To My Enemy, 2004

My manuscripts,
Read upon your folded knees, one page per breath,
Then discarded into the grave of books.
Though I wagered all of my youth,
I could surrender myself joyfully,
Because it was you seated before me;
Snow fell softly by the window,
The third pot of tea cooled.
You, the only one before me—
But I am choked by the paradise of shadows,
By those beautiful, dreamlike days
When I aligned even my gestures and voice with yours.
I will now banish the stranger, the not-me, within.
I have split my belly within a flowerpot,
And before the purple wildflower, overgrown in its pot,
    withers,
I will cast seeds to the wind and scatter them in the
    field.
If I cannot reach your depth,
If I measure myself by your standards,
I will not torment myself like this any longer.
To the one who merely stirs within,
I wish to grant the courage and freedom to bloom alone.
O my enemy, watching over my shoulder!

I am but small brown seeds,
Drifting through fleeting moments of life.
I will be scattered asunder—
Beside fluttering wings of descending sparrows,
No, within a lingering breath blown across the globe,
In another's hand, toward the void.
I will unfurl my white, downy parachute
And fly to wherever the moonlight rises.
Through the three or four typhoons that arrive each
      year,
I may live as a weed,
Growing tall, feathered leaves, speckled with dirt.
Thus, to you outside me,
And to the you beyond you,
May I listen, learn by ear, in the lowest stance.
Forgive me, O my enemy, whom I already miss—
How swiftly I've seized the reckless liberty
To love myself this way!

그늘 한 칸의 골상학, 2024

그늘 속에서
당신의 뒷모습을 본다
푸름을 안은 나무
한낮의 불볕 먼저 삭이고서
내겐 오직 연둣빛을 흘려준다
잎을 지나 묽어지는 빛
모이고 갈라지는 수천 잎맥이
당신의 담론을 이어간다
그늘 속에 있다는 것은
잠시 누군가의 품속에 있다는 것
나뭇가지들이 두런두런 어깨를 내준다
떠난 것은 새겨지고
남은 것은 뭉근하다
이면(裏面)이
지등(紙燈)을 켠다
작열하는 광명에 응하여
속 불을 지피는 수천 창호(窓戶)
당신의 골상학이 완성되고 있다
스며서 번져오는 빛
어찌 탄화되어 저리 은은한 것일까
제 발치를 서늘히 품는
세상 모든 당신에게
홍복(洪福)이 있을진저
당신의 그늘 밖으로 나가는 때
나도 작은 그늘 한 칸 데리고 가리니

Phrenology of a Shaded Haven, 2024

In the shade,
I see your figure from behind—
A tree enveloped in green,
First absorbing the scorching midday sun,
Then casting a soft, greenish light upon me.
Light mellows as it filters through the leaves,
Whose veins, converging and diverging in a thousand
    ways,
Continue your eloquent discourse.
To be in the shade is
To be within someone's embrace for a time.
The whispering branches offer shoulders to lean upon.
What has passed is etched;
What remains, settled and steady.
The other sides light their paper lanterns.
Your phrenology nears completion,
As thousands of leaf panes kindle inner lights
Against the incandescent brightness.
Light, seeping and submerging—
How subtly it refines, like charring.
May great blessings be upon those
Who coolly bear their own steps.
One day, as I step out of your shade,
I, too, will carry.
A small shaded haven within me.

발문
나의 삶과 시를 위한 소론

일의 시작은 결단을 요구한다. 이 결단은 시작의
의지를 하나로 굳히는 것을 뜻하기도 하지만, 다른
한편으로는 스스로의 역량의 부족함과 제약을
받아들이는 것을 뜻하기도 한다.

-김우창, 《궁핍한 시대의 시인》, 5.

Epilogue
Apologia Pro Vita Mea et Poesi

The beginning of any endeavor demands determination. This determination not only signifies solidifying one's will to commence but also implies accepting one's limitations and constraints.

—Uchang Kim, *Poets in a Destitue Time*, 5.

발문: 나의 삶과 시를 위한 소론

나는 둘이 아니다. 어떻게든 하나다. 저녁 새 떼처럼 통합의 욕구 속에 숲 어귀로 돌아온다. 나는 당신이 그러하듯 하나의 실체이기 위해 언제 어디서나 긴장한다. 현실이 있다. 이에 굴복하든 무시하든 혹 제대로 싸웠다고 착각하든 현실은 상존한다. 그 안에 내가 있다. 아래 혹은 위에 있을 수도 있으나 그 속에 있다. 현실이 또 하나의 실체를 이룬다. 현실과 나 사이에는 완충지대가 없다. 잠들지 않는 한 사방이 전장이다. 어쩌면 꿈속에서 더 치열하게 싸운다. 각자의 실질을 유지하는 두 개의 실체가 붙어산다. 일 대하기 일, 그 양립의 위상은 각자가 상대에 종속되지 않는다는 전제에서 허용된다. 대립은 갈등을 부른다. 한쪽이 다른 쪽을 정복하려 한다.

나에게 시는 두 성격의 일이 결합하여 다시 일이 되어가는 중립지대의 흔적이다. 시는 현실보다 크거나 작을 수 있다. 시는 나보다 높거나 낮을 수 있다. 하지만 시는 현실과 나를 어떤 방식으로든 하나로 묶는다. 그 통합이 덧셈이 아니라 뺄셈의 방식에 따를 때도 시는 단순한 증감을 넘어 새롭게 다른 실체를 이룬다. 일 빼기 일이 영이 아니라 다시 일이 되는 이유가 여기에 있다. 나는 현실을 벗어난 적이 없다. 내게 시는 "반올림"이든 "반(牛)-내림"이든 현실과 내가 벌여온 옥신각신의 결과로서 늘 그 자리에서 새로운 현실을 이룬다.

그랬으면 한다.

시는 삶이다: 1+1=1

시는 머리에서 나오지 않는다. 시는 가슴에서 기원하지 않는다. 이 부정의 나열은 시가 그 모두에서 탄생한다고 말하려는 것일 수 있다. 시는 시인에게 총체적 역량의 결집을 요구하기 때문이다. 하지만 이 언급들에 빠진 게 있다. 시의 형성에 핵심적으로 작용하는데도 간과되는 것이 있다. 어쩌면 너무 당연해서 눈에 띄지 않는 것인지 모른다. 그것은 시가 현실에 대한 상상력의 산물이라는 사실이다. 이 진술에서 방점은 상상력뿐만 아니라 현실에도 찍혀 있다. 시는 정신의 작용 없이는 생산될 수 없다. 그런데 그 정신은 현실에 긴밀하게 조응하는 관계를 통해서 가장 큰 활력을 띤다. 정신의 활동을 촉발하고 시에 없어서는 안 될 현실, 그것은 무엇인가?

세상 그 자체가 현실이다. 과연 그럴까? 세상은 내가 보는 대로, 느끼는 대로, 생각하는 대로, 존재한다. 우리가 수용하고 표현하는 세상은 우리가 그렇다고 보고, 느끼고, 생각하는 세상이다. 세상은 구성체인 셈이다. 구성의 핵심적 요소는 세상 그 자체다. 그리고 이에 버금갈 핵심적 요소로서 그것을 파악하는 자의 의식이 있다. 세상의 구성에는 두 가지 기본 요소에 더하여 문화, 전통, 이념, 제도 등이 관여할 수 있다. 그 구성체에 대한 인간의 개입이 자기중심에 치우칠수록 세상은 더 아름다워지거나 더 추해질 수 있다. 심지어 세상 그 자체의 흔적이 거의 사라질 수도 있다. 세상이 구성의 방식으로 존재한다면 그 최상의 방식은 무엇일까?

세상은 현실이고 시는 상상력이다. 이 통상적 이분법은 시와 세상이 실제로 존재하는 방식을 왜곡한다. 이 왜곡에서 세상에는 의식이 배제되어 있고 시에는 세상이 배제되어 있다. 실제에서 세상은 의식을 통해 드러나고 그것을 표현하는 시에는 세상이 담겨 있다. 세상과 시 모두는 같은 원리로 구성된다. 세상이 의식의 구성체이고 시가 그것을 표현하는 한 그러하다. 둘 다 세상과 의식의 융합을 구현한다.

229

상상력은 세상의 복잡성을 존중하는 총체적 정신 능력이다. 삶의 구체적 세부와 상호반응하는 상상력에서 세상은 그 가치가 최대로 발현된다. 이러한 여건이 허용되는 작은 시공에서 세상의 구조는 시의 구조를 이룬다. 현실이 사실적이면서 또한 비사실적인 양상을 발현하는 시의 마을에서 삶은 시이고 시는 삶이다.

현실은 켜켜이 쌓여 가는 퇴적층이다. 그 가장 깊은 곳에는 아마도 "화병에 꽃이 꽂혀 있지 않다는 걸" 아무렇지도 않게 받아들이는 정오 혹은 오후가 "무수히 만개한 안개꽃 소수점들"로 찍혀 있을 것이다. "그런 찰나들이 침상에 쌓여 푹신하게" 느껴지는 날 누군가는 "솥 바닥 긁어대는 쇠숟가락 소리"를 듣는다. 그는 "사라져간 영혼"과 날마다 무사한 어느 하루 사이에 갇혀 있다(〈나는 날마다 가출한다〉).

하루는 "수평으로 돌아가는 자전의 각도"에서 "삼시세끼가 진저리 처지는 무량한 수렁"이고 "알맞게 늙은 얼굴을 내미는 당신의 저체온 같은 그런 무탈한 환장"이다(〈내가 나를 보듬는 날〉). "온 데서 와서 / 간 데로 가는 / 가로수 직립보행"에서 도로는 바로 현실의 얼굴이다(〈별일 없는 나날의 일지〉). 안전을 도모하는 신호등은 "항상 제로에서 안색을" 바꾸고 연속무늬 보도블록은 더불어 이동하는 리듬의 토대를 이루지만 그 "이음매 속에 숨어 사는 모서리"는 "갈라서자 바로 날을 세우는 각도"를 날카롭게 드러낸다(〈카운트다운〉).

현실은 개인이 통제할 수 없는 외적 세력에 종속되어 있다. 우리는 자본주의가 지배하는 자유 민주주의 대한민국에 살고 있다. 이 문장의 자간에는 역사적, 사회적, 문화적, 정치적, 경제적 사건들이 소용돌이치고 있다. 닫아걸고 살아도 우리의 창과 문은 광장을 향해 있다. 우리는 현실을 구성하는 맥락적 요소를 최우선에 내세우지 않는 때도 그에 저절로 노출되고 반응한다. 우리는 "목마름으로 외쳤던 그녀의 가두방송"을 기억한다. 1980년 5월 광주의 기억에서 오늘 우리가 누리는 것의 가치가 누군가의 헌신과 피의 대가라는 사실은 자명하다. 하지만 기차는 먼저 떠난 자, 살아남은 자, 자기 앞의 생을 살아가는 자를 싣고 직진할 뿐이다(〈오월이 오면〉).

왜 역사는 실수를 반복하는 것일까? 있어서는 안 되는 일이 탐욕의 결과로 일어났고 여전히 반복된다. 오늘도 세상은 어디선가 "정거장을 덮치는 아파트"에 깔려 "버스 뒷자리에 압사하는 귀가"가 있을 듯하고 "바람에 흔들리는 대교"가 발아래 한강으로 꺼질 듯하다. 또한 누군가 "시퍼런 물속에서 보내온 마지막 문자"를 당장이라도 열어볼 듯하다(〈아주 오래된 오늘〉). 현실은 이렇게 "멀어지는 자의 항적에서 부옇게 일어나 / 따라가는 자의 창에 뿌려지는 분무"처럼 위태롭게 우리를 에워싼다(〈빗길에 운전 중〉).

현실의 퇴적층은 표층에 가까울수록 더 구체적이고 더 단단한 삶의 세부를 드러낸다. 일상은 아침저녁으로 부딪는 장면이고 사건이다. 신비하지도 아름답지도 않다. 그 표층에서 지하로 꺼지지 않으려면 부력(浮力)이 필요하다. 먼 데를 바라보거나 가까이 익숙한 것에 새 숨결을 불어넣어야 한다. 시 〈바질〉에서 "엄마의 생애와 딸의 일생"은 화자가 "날마다 직면해야 하는 현실의 두 세부"를 구성한다. 〈소띠 그대〉에서 현실은 오랜 세월 함께 살아온 아내의 낯섦이다. "그대"는, 이제껏 안다고 생각했으나, 너무 친숙해 심지어 잊고 지냈으나, 어느 순간 더는 어떤 이름으로도 불러낼 수 없는 존재로 부상한다. 아내는 "엄마, 자네, 여보 / 그따위 통칭의 얼개에서 모질게 빠져나와 / 갓 터지려 입술을 삐죽 내미는 / 천년의 딸"로 변신한다. 현실은 익숙해질수록 낯설어지는 속성을 품는다. 현실은 만남과 헤어짐이 무수히 반복되는 시공이다. 그래서일 것이다. 묵은 현실에서는 수천 번의 생각과 느낌이 석양 후 어스름처럼 지나온 세월 쪽으로 켜켜이 일렁여 흑백으로 추상화된다.

두 갈래 길이 나란히 따로 간다: 당신

나는 길에 있고, 길 밖의 길에, 삶의 언저리에, 당신, 그대, 너로 대변되는 반(反)중력의 존재들이 있다. 다들 그러하듯 나도 인생길을 따라간다. 그 길에서 멀리 혹 가까이 날 이끄는 듯한 혹은 따라오는 듯한 이들과 함께 걷는다. 함께 걸어도 같은 길에 있지는 않다. 가지 않은 길이 나란히 이어진다. 각자의 길에 있는 우리는 이쪽과 저쪽에서 앞서거니 뒤서거니 걷다가 어느새 동반자가 되었다. 현실은 비현실과 부대끼다가 서로 닮는다. 현실은 비현실에 의해 열망을 유지하고 비현실은 현실에 의해 두 발을 땅에 딛는다. 현실과 비현실이 융합한 또 하나의 현실, 시는 이것을 구현한다. 일 플러스 일이 다시 일이 되는 방식에서 현실은 상상적인 것이 되고 상상력은 현실적인 것이 된다.

"당신"은 환유와 은유로 이뤄진 한 권의 시집이다. 시집은 누군가의 한 세월이 농축된 곳이다. 화자는 그 곁에 다가서고자 아니 그 품에 안기고자 그에 뜨거운 한잔의 커피로 엎질러진다. 커피에 젖어 갈색으로 뒤틀리는 시집은 "간헐천이라도 곧장 치솟을 듯 / 뒤틀린 어느 화산지형"을 이룬다. 그런데 어쩐지 그 당신은 시가 그러하듯 환유와 은유가 그러하듯 흐릿하다. 당신은 세상사 삭여 꼭꼭 품은 듯 "관계의 접점마저 다듬어져 가려지는" 몸짓으로 있다. 그런 당신을 향해 화자는 함께 웅크릴 것을 고대한다. 이런 당신이란 혹 화자가 불러낸 자신 또는 그가 써낸 시의 세계가 아닐까. "자세를 유지하고 제때 물러서던" 그이는 혹 "바람의 저쪽으로 머쓱하게 흩어지는" 화자의 뒷모습이 아닐까(〈당신이라는 환유〉).

"당신"은 시 쓰는 행위 자체를 가리킬 수 있다. 그 만성적 습관의 징

후가 "방치의 펜촉"에서 "흰 녹"으로 여실해지는 순간에서 화자는 "영원한 자기복제의 저주"에 갇힌다. 여기서 화자는 "너라는 원점에서 시작하는 나라는 맹점"을 확인하면서 글쓰기의 불편을 토로하고 있기도 하다. 시 쓰기가 기원하는 너는 길 밖에 있고 나는 길 위에 있다. 당신은 끊임없이 일깨우고 손짓하나 나는 그에 이르지 못한다. 함께 가고 있으나 그 간격이 좁혀지지 않는다(〈지상의 오랜 명사들〉).

그 손아귀에서 벗어날 수 없다고 느껴지는 어떤 것을 대하는 때가 있다. 그것은 영혼을 짓누르는 삶의 무게일 때가 있으나 그 무게에 저항하도록 나를 받쳐주는 반중력일 때도 있다. 현실은 피하기 어렵고 극복기는 더 힘들다. 시를 쓰는 행위는 이러한 현실에 대한 맞섬 혹은 균형의 시도이다. 시는 "멀리 고이는 것"에 자라는 "푸른 / 심도"와 "세상 소음" 사이에서 시소를 탄다. 내 대부분 시에 기본적인 동력을 제공하는 감정의 율동과 사고의 흐름은 이러한 역학을 따라가고 있다. "학수고대해도 강림하지 않다가 / 저 안에서 쑤시듯 아려오는 놈"이나 "내 삶의 뒤안길에 / 보일 듯 말 듯 따라다니는 녀석"은 어쩌다 시를 가져다주는 자로서 나의 수호자이다. 나는 흠칫 "바람의 빈손"을 받아들이는 체념의 달인이었다가 초월적 시선을 멀리 보내는 구도자였다가 다시 하산하여 "네 갈래 오이소박이"를 탐닉하는 현실주의자의 자세를 취한다. 시 쓰기의 박자가 삶을 추동하는 리듬에 맞춰져 있다. 그 흐름에서 벗어날 수 없으므로 시 쓰기는 운명이고, 시는 길 가장자리의 동반자이다(〈동행〉).

"당신"은 자신과 마주하는 고독의 순간을 지칭할 수도 있다. 혼자의 시간에 내적으로 직면하는 것은 관찰과 사유의 대상으로 객체화된다. 평생 함께해온 "가지 않은 길이 일으키는 현기증"은 나의 동반자로서 당신의 인격을 획득한다(〈쓸쓸〉). 시끄러운 카페 구석에서 저물 무렵 들판으로 마음의 문이 열리는 "작은 신의 공간"에서 고립을 감내하는 자는 사방을 향해 열리는 "네 귀의 나"에 도달한다. 길에서 길 밖의 당신을 만나는 순간이 이렇듯 쫑긋할 것이다(〈오후의 목신〉).

뒤로 비틀거려 앞으로 걷는다: 자세

갈팡질팡 살아온 듯해도 세월은 어디론가 방향을 잡고 있다. 몸인지 마음인지 어느 깊은 곳의 부름에 응하는 때가 있다. 그런 순간이 간헐적으로 이어지다가 아예 그림자처럼 붙어 다니기도 한다. 때로는 그에 저항하였으나 때로는 그에 부응하여 살아온, 어느 길이 보인다. 반복하여 저지르는 실수가 있다. 그 실수가 나를 나답게 만들어준다고 자신을 옹호하게 되는 역설의 완성에서 나는 나만의 길에 들어선다. 모종의 자세와 먼 지향점이 시에 자주 등장하는 것은 흐릿하게 명멸하는 운명을 예지하고 차라리 예정하려는 욕구 탓일 것이다.

발바닥의 접점이 발길을 이룬다. 그 길에서 가장자리 끝이나 그 너머를 응시하는 데서 시가 시작한다. 가까이 있어도 잡히지 않고 멀리 있어도 사라지지 않는 지향점이 있다. 부재의 현존 혹은 현존의 부재에서 화자는 언젠가 자신이 마른 풀처럼 "청춘을 소환해줄 모든 것을 잃고 / 종(種)의 기원을 잊고 / 이름마저" 벗어버린 "순수한 껍질"이 될 것을 예감한다. "일몰의 등고선"에서 바람길을 쓸고 있는 마른 풀대 밭을 마주하여 화자는 "강철의 빗살무늬"가 자신에게 "회초리를 쳐드는" 환상에 빠진다. 화자에게 "환하게" 가해지는 회초리는 마지막 순간까지 바람길을 지키는 자세를 그에게 가르친다(〈금악행〉).

길에서 길 밖을 기웃거리는 자는 "느티나무 잎이 일으키는 수천무음 진동을 / 부드럽게 쓸고 가는 무심으로" 대하고자 하고(〈저 흰소 떼〉) 차창 풍경에 흔들리다가 "종아리 드러낸 한 소년"이 되어 "백사장 / 도도하게 흐르는 은빛 속으로" 사라지고자 한다(〈백사장 은빛 속으로〉). 그는 산 정상에 올라 "이름이나마 지워 버릴까 궁리하면서"(〈하산을 미루다〉) 미장원 거울 앞에서는 "잘라도 멋대로 다시 자라는" 것을 "그믐밤 삭발하는 돌중"이 되어 털어내고 싶어 한다(〈무명초〉).

자신을 다독이고 추스르는 자세는 부정하고 비우는 자세와 맞물리기 마련이다. 길 위의 수행자는 "시원하게 비 쏟아지기 직전의 탁한 여백 속으로" 느긋하게 "묻혀가는 뒷모습"을 보여주려 한다(((〈흐리고 바람 부는 날은〉). 그의 시선은 수직의 높이가 아니라 수평의 균등을 향해 있다. 하지만 동시에 그는 길 위에 곧추서 있기도 하다. "깨금발로 서서 더 멀리 보려는 나 / 마냥 서 있으려는 나"는 "풀밭의 심전도"가 그라운드 제로에 그리는 직선과 마주하여 반성의 자세를 취한다. "기껏해야 순간의 중심을 견디는 나"의 직립보행이 "길게 널브러진 십 리 들길"에서 트라우마와 마주한다. 늘 곤두선 자신과 다 내려놓은 들판 사이에서 수행자는 그만 눕고 싶어 하는 듯하다(〈그라운드 제로〉). "후배에게 주장을 펼쳤고 / 선배에게 무능을 가장(假裝)했다"라는 후회에서 그는 길 밖을 향하고 있다(〈어제도 많은 말을 했다〉). 두 발의 접점을 따라 걷고 있으나 "눈꺼풀은 닫고 / 부처 귀는 열어두는 / 허허심처"의 마음을 키우고 있다(〈동행〉).

정은 누룩 빛이다: 사랑

여전히 철없는 낭만주의자일 줄 모른다고 흠칫 자각하는 때가 있다. 흔들자 흐려졌다가 반투명 누룩 빛으로 서서히 맑아지는 곡주, 애정이 익는 모습이 그러하다. 현실의 혼돈이 시간의 체에 걸러지고 발효되어 다소 불순하게 추출되는 미량의 정수(精髓), 그것이 사랑이고 그래서 시이다.

기억은 "끓고 휘돌고 우러나고 가라앉고 / 밋밋하게 식어가는 찻물"

이다. "싹 치운 후 아직 아무것도 펼쳐지지 않은 / 아침 마당"에서 차 한 잔으로 시작하는 하루는 평화롭다. 찻잔에서 "남몰래 간직한 사랑의 신맛"과 "찻잎이 녹여낸 언덕 햇살"이 녹아 나온다. 꼬이고 엮인 시간이 그렇게 풀어질 수 있으면 좋으리라(〈찻물 식어가는 소리〉).

시간이 꼭 앞으로 가지는 않는다. 사람과 사람이 꼭 다른 삶을 살지는 않는다. 당신의 얼굴 안에 "당신보다 더 당신을 걱정했을 누군가"가 살고 "소파에 묻힌 아내의 귀밑"에서 "장모님의 흰머리"가 자란다(〈문을 열어두고 향을 피우네〉). "그 여름이 어느 여름으로 / 다시 아무 여름이나로" 흘러가는 시간의 물길 가장자리에서 "모든 햇살이 당신을 가리키는 아침"이 열리고 "모든 그림자가 당신을 호위하는 저녁"이 저문다(〈반올림〉). "쉰내가 풍기는" 기억에서 "간혹 주정 꽃이 피는" 때는 내 안의 소년이 "우다방 계단"에 앉아 "돌아오지 않는 강"을 부른다(〈후후〉).

가족은 감상주의에 치우질 위험에 노출된 시적 제재이나 현실주의자의 심미적 탐색에 제법 효과적인 입구를 열어준다. 가족은 희로애락이 숙성되는 시적 현실이다. 그 문을 슬쩍 열고 다른 세상을 넘보기에 이만한 입구가 드물다. 〈커피 한 잔과 사과 한 톨의 라르고〉에서 사랑은 "묵은내가 진동하는 김치냉장고"에서 "사과 두 톨을 찾아내는 짓"이다. 그런데 화자는 사과 두 개를 "접시 두 개에 나란히 따로 올려놓고" "헝클어진 서랍에 숨은 / 노란 손잡이의 과도를 꺼내 칼날을 벼르는 짓"마저 사랑에 포함하고 있다. 사랑은 낭만의 소산이 아니라 갈등과 조정의 결과일 수 있다. 사과 껍질을 벗기는 데도 두 가지 방식이 존재한다. 여섯 조각으로 등분한 후 깎는 법과 통째로 돌려가면서 깎는 법이 공존한다. 사랑은 활활 타오르는 연소가 아니라 "차갑고 단단한 속살을 한 조각씩 고백하는 / 과육의 나열을 다시 배열하는 짓"이어서 대화와 타협이 필요하다. 현실은 지옥도 아니고 천국도 아니다. 그렇다고 연옥인 것도 아니어서 천국은 요원하고 언제든 지옥으로 떨어질 수 있다. 지상의 삶을 수용하면서 그 안에서 잠깐, 아름답다, 조용히 뇌까릴 수 있게 해주는 힘, 그런 것이 사랑이고 시이다.

생각과 감정은 발효한다. 무르익은 것은 추상을 발현한다. 이것이 현실의 양상이다. 일 더하기 일이나 일 빼기 일이 다시 일이 되는 일이 일어난다. 삶에서 시가 발생한다. 몸과 마음에 들어왔다 나가는 것은 무엇이든 흔적을 새긴다. 흔적의 퇴적은 견고하지 않다. 쌓인 것은 간혹 빗물에 휩쓸린다. 다수의 각도와 꼭짓점이 깎이고 씻겨 시간의 강 언저리에 토사로 쌓이면서 공명의 공식이 완성된다. 삶의 가장자리에는 생각이나 감정만이지는 않고 그렇다고 사물뿐이지만은 않는 것들이 살고 있다. 몸과 마음은 공명이 진동하는 곳이다. 시집이란 이러한 삶의 테두리를 따라가는 공명의 집일 것이다.

일상은 형이상, 형이상은 일상이다: 시론

낭만과 관념은 현실에 맞설 힘이 부족하다, 이것은 벽을 향해 나지막이 읊조리는 나의 화두이다. 현실에 맞설 반(反)현실의 존재는 현실처럼 실체적 근력을 지녀야 한다. 시인은 현실 안에서 그에 맞설 힘을 구해야 하지 않을까. 반(反)중력은 중력을 거스르는 힘이지 무(無)중력이 아니다. 시가 추구하는 자유는 초월이 아니라 짓누르는 힘이 약해지거나 상쇄되는 상태일 것이다. 지상의 시인은 신 대신에 정신에 의존하되 자의적 중심에 함몰하지 않고 현실을 존중하되 그 위압에 눌리지 않는다. 이렇게 작동하는 정신은 반중력의 활력을 띠나 현실을 왜곡하거나 미화하지 않는다. 이러한 정신의 활동은 시에 어떻게 드러날 수 있을까. 그 정신에 의해 인식되고 구성되어 재현되는 현실은 삶에서 그리고 시에서 어떻게 드러날 수 있을까.

정신의 활력, 이것이 우리가 기댈 수 있는 마지막 언덕이다. 정신은 어떻게 최선으로 활성화될 수 있는가. 엘리엇(T. S. Eliot)은 앞선 시대의 "감수성의 분열"을 비판하면서 생각과 감정의 재통합을 중시했다. 역사적으로 정신 활동의 요체가 감정의 힘 쪽에 치우친 적이 있었고 사유의 힘 쪽에 쏠린 적이 있었다. 생각과 감정의 이분법에서 양자는 물과 기름처럼 섞이지 않는다. 이성적 사유가 보편적 가치를 추구할 때 주관적 감정과 개인적 독특성의 가치는 억압된다. 논리와 사실의 한계를 넘어가는 감정의 능력에서 세상은 다채로워지고 심원해지나 동시에 객체성을 잃을 수 있다. 이성과 보편을 중시했던 18세기, 상상력과 독창을 내세웠던 19세기, 인본주의적 양극단의 폐해를 극복하고자 감수성의 통합을 꾀했던 20세기, 이러한 역사적 흐름에서 21세기의 글쓰기는 어떤 출구를 마련하고 있을까.

절대자가 사라진 세상에서 각자의 차이를 인정하면서 전체의 조화를 유지하는 데는 객체성의 존중이 필수적이다. 그 객체의 세상은 정신을 통해 구성되지 않는 한 드러날 수 없다. 정신의 활동은 어떻게 세상을 존중의 방식으로 의식화할 수 있는가. 생각과 감정이 동시에 작동하여 두 가치를 살리면서 또한 각자의 한계를 보완하는 일은 어떻게 이뤄질 수 있을까. 이런 거대 담론이 시인의 실제 글쓰기에서 어떻게 실증적으로 구현될 수 있을까.

워즈워스(William Wordsworth)는 1800년 ≪서정민요시집≫ 제2판 서문에서 시의 정의를 내리는 가운데 흥미롭게도 생각과 감정이 전통적 이분법을 넘어서는 관계에 대해 언급하였다. 그에 따르면 훌륭한 시는 "힘센 느낌이 저절로 넘쳐흐른 것"이다. 그런데 이 감정은 날 것이 아니라 숙고의 과정을 통해 다듬어진 것이라는 데 주목할 필요가 있다. "생각에 따라 수정되는" 감정의 세련은 지난 경험에 관한 통찰에서 빚어진다. 여기서 "여러 생각은 실로 과거 모든 감정의 대표자들이다." 시인은 이러한 "감정의 대표자들" 사이의 관계를 숙고함으로써 "인간에게 진정으로 중요한 것이 무엇인지"를 깨닫고 그 행위를 반복하게 된다. 이러한 "유기적 감수성"에서 두 능력은 상호영향을 끼치고 서로를 수정하는 관계에서 분리할 수 없는 일체를 이룬다.

그렇지만 생각과 느낌은 실제로 어떻게 하나가 될 수 있는가. 그 융합의 균형은 어떤 방식에서 최선에 달할 수 있는가. 워즈워스의 "유기적 감수성"과 엘리엇이 말하는 "감수성"은 비슷한 듯 다르다. 엘리엇에게 감수성의 분열과 통합은 일차적으로 시대적 추이를 뜻하였으나 워즈워스에게 그것은 창조 과정의 개인적 현상이었다. 워즈워스의 시는 교훈적 어조가 강한 경우가 잦다. 그가 천명한 시의 정의는 감정의 우위를 허용하는 듯하나 그 감정은 워즈워스 자신의 개인주의적이고 이상적인 사유에 수정되는 종류의 것이었다. 그의 시가 아름다운 자연의 형상으로 가득한 이유가 여기에 있다. 이에 비하여 엘리엇이 시인의 자질로서 요구하는 감수성은 삶의 경험이 총체적으로 관여하여 자연스럽게 길러지는 무의식적 능력을 뜻하였다.

워즈워스의 "유기적 감수성"은 낭만주의자의 개인적 사유에 의존한다. 엘리엇의 감수성의 통합은 개성을 배제하는 모더니스트의 접근법에 따른다. 워즈워스의 감정이 주관적 사유를 거쳐 숭고하게 고양되는 양상과 다르게 엘리엇의 그것은 "대상, 상황, 사건" 등과 같은 "객관적 상관물"의 거리두기를 통해 간접적으로 환기되는 데 그친다.

윌리엄스(William Carlos Williams)의 이미지즘은 파운드(Ezra Pound)가 비판했던 "감정의 미끄러짐"에 대한 지적 통제의 정신을 구현한다. 정확한 이미지의 언어를 제시하는 일은 자기중심적 세계의 구성에 저항한다. 상징으로 넘어가지 않는 이미지의 단단함은 사물에 인간에게 종속되지 않는 자유를 주면서 인간을 사물의 주인이 아니라 관찰자적 동반자의 위치로 물러서게 한다. "관념은 사물 속에서만 존재한다"라는 그의 금언은 세상을 있는 그대로의 아름다움으로 수용하려는 의도적 시도를 드러낸다. 세상이 어떻게든 사유와 감정을 통해 재구성될 수밖에 없는 불가피한 여건에서 윌리엄스는 전체의 맥락 대신에 부분에 그리고 시간의 연속 대신에 순간의 불연속적 전환에 집중함으로써 관념의 통세에서 벗어난 사물을 창조하고자 하였다. 그는 시인의 정신이 사물들 사이의 동일성 대신에 그 차별성을 분간하는 때 최대치로 활성화된다고 보았다.

정신은 감수성의 통합에서 활력을 띤다. 이렇게 그 중요성을 강조하기는 쉬우나 그것의 성취가 어떻게 이뤄져야 하는가에 대해 답하기는 쉽지 않다. 영미 시의 역사에서 주요 시인마다 다른 접근법을 보여준다. 우리 시대에 어울리는 시인의 정신은 현실에 맞서 어떻게 작용해야 하는가? 한 예로서 21세기 미국 시인 그레이엄(Jorie Graham)은 그녀의 시에서 대상에 대한 즉각적 반응과 의식적 불신의 역학을 극화한다. 예민한 지각을 활짝 열어놓은 가운데 사유가 발동하나 한순간의 결론에 얽매이지 않고 끊임없이 무너지고 세워지면서 다음의 인식을 향해 나간다. 부정의 정신은 파괴보다 건설에 방점을 찍는다. 끝내 완성될 수 없는 깨달음을 향해서 연속적으로 주춧돌을 새롭게 세우는 긴장에서 현실은 환상으로 환상은 다시 현실로 일렁인다.

내 시적 취향과 기질은 영미 시의 다양하고 방대한 정전에서 이러한 흐름을 따라 길러졌다. 엄밀하게 단단하게 글을 쓰려는 자세는 영미 비평의 숲을 헤쳐나오면서 몸에 배게 된 습성이다. 첫 시집부터 지금까지 발견되는 내 시의 몸짓에서 꼭 나만의 것인 것은 아닌 저들의 표정이 보인다. 시를 쓰는 순간은 현실에 맞서는 순간이다. 워즈워스, 엘리엇, 윌리엄스, 그레이엄을 위시한 지상의 시인은 자신의 방식으로 반중력을 실현한다. 이 섬세한 균형에서 삶의 세부는 간혹 형이상적 빛을 발한다. 일상은 형이상이고 형이상은 일상이다, 자주 되새겨보는 나의 시론이다.

시에서 감정은 사유에 의해 수정되고 방향성이 주어진다. 생각과 느낌의 접선을 따라 일상은 형이상이 되고 형이상은 범상해진다. 창가 화분에서 "앞섶을 하얗게 열어버리는 꽃"은 "살짝 헤픈 여자"를 상기시켜 "싫다가 좋다가 미워지다가" "그냥 친구"로 남는다. 서너 해 바지런하게 꽃을 피우더니 "올봄 내내 꽃 소식이 없"는 그런 친구 곁에서 화자는 "제발 아프지만 말라고" 중얼거리고 있다(〈재스민〉).

일상에서 우리가 가장 가까이 대하는 것은 혼자이다. 혼자와 마주하는 시간이 현실의 세부를 이룬다. 피할 수 없어서 조용히 지켜보다가 우리는 서서히 그와 친해진 나머지 자신의 일부로 수용하게 된다. 혼자라는 느낌은 숨결과 같아서 우리가 마주하는 세상에 정령처럼 깃들게 된다. 고독은 나뿐만 아니라 "세상 모든 것의 허파에 잠입하여 / 세상 모든 것의 핏줄기를 타고 흘러가는" 기생적 존재로 파악된다(〈쓸쓸〉). 사물이 쓸쓸함의 덧옷을 걸쳐 입고 있다. 고독은 나도 사물도 벗어날 수 없는 삶의 전제(前提)인 셈이다. 나에게 서정은 사유의 대상으로 관찰되고 자조적 깨달음의 대상으로 화한다. 서정은 쏟아지는 듯해도 관찰되고 목격되는 듯해도 안에서 솟는다. 시인은 고독을 토로하는 자가 아니라 고독에 관해 사유하는 자이다.

풀에서 꽃이 핀다. 어디에 시선을 두느냐에 따라 꽃이기도 하고 풀이기도 하다. 성숙한다는 것은 풀이 꽃으로 발전하는 것이리라. 유월, 백합꽃 나팔 소리에 넋을 놓는다. 풀에서 돋은 꽃이 무리를 지어 "떡갈나무 영토를 건너가는 징검다리"를 놓는다. 꽃은 "맘을 고하는 몸"으로서 "한 여름으로 가는 길의 음향과 분노"를 집적한다. 뜻을 품고 "세상에 나선 지상의 딸들"이다. 꽃에는 꽃말이 뒤따른다. "꽃잎 세 장의 상징"은 순수다. 그따위 것은 "폐교의 화단에 꽂힌 나무 팻말"에 불과하니 "꽃말은 말끔히 잊고" "흰 꽃의 향이 이끄는 대로" 춤출지어다(〈꽃말에 관한 속말〉).

시는 서정적이다. 하지만 서정에 과다 노출되어 온 탓인지, 익숙한 서정에 항체가 생겨서인지, 서정 자체보다 그 서정에 대한 사유에서, 그 언어의 쓰임새에서, 신선함을 찾게 된다. 세상이 너무 많은 진리로 시끄러운 탓인지 구도의 시에서 만나는 깨달음에 역반응이 자주 일어난다. 진리의 현시보다 오히려 그것의 부재에서 혹은 그것을 지향하는 부정의 움직임에서, 그 움직임을 지향하는 자아와 언어의 율동에서, 더 큰 각성의 마력을 느낀다. 서정은 서정에 대한 사유로 그리고 진리는 진리를 향한 움직임으로 대체된다. 오늘 나의 시는 그랬으면 싶다.

삶은 대치이거나 당착이다: 균형

시는 나에게 스티븐스의 정의대로 "삶의 어느 특별한 세부가 아주 오랫동안 생각되어온 나머지 생각이 그것의 분리할 수 없는 한 부분이 되어버린 것이거나 아주 강렬하게 느껴진 나머지 느낌이 그 안에 들어가 있는 어떤 것이다." 이 정의는 시에 고유의 영토를 따로 허용하는 시론을 제시하지 않고 주변에서 실제 일어나는 일을 정확하게 표현한다. "세상에는 사실적인 것과 비사실적인 상상의 것이 너무 닮아서 서로 분간할 수 없는 것들로 밀집해 있다." 이런 현실의 세부가 "삶의 매우 중요한 경험의 한 부분"이라는 스티븐스의 인식이 나의 궁핍한 시론의 밑거름이다.

예전에는 깨닫지 못했으나 요즘 새록새록 일어나는 새 흥분이 있다. 그것은 시 쓰는 기교나 언어의 재치에서가 아니라 삶의 인식이나 자세에서 발생한다. 현실을 무시할 수도 무조건 수용할 수도 그 너머로 나갈 수도 없다. 삶에는 언제나 이념과 현실이 충돌하고 타협한다. 인간사는 무수한 층위의 명암을 품는다. 어떻게 휘젓느냐에 따라 무수한 추상이 이뤄진다. 낭만, 관념, 이상은 현실 너머에 있기도 하고 그 안에 있기도 하다. 그것이 현실 속에 들어와 존재하는 절충, 타협, 균형의 방식은 경우마다 다르다. 그 추이를 감지하고 좇아가는 능력에서 시인은 개별적이고 독창적이다.

내 시에서 찻물 식어가는 소리를 품은 찻잔, 거실 창가의 재스민, 냉장고 옆 탁자에 거꾸로 서 있는 요거트 병, "반내림"의 저물 무렵 들판 등은 생각과 느낌이 너무 오래 그곳에 머물러서 그것의 일부가 되어 있다. 그것은 현실이면서 비현실이다. 이렇게 시적 공간으로 화하는 삶의 터전에서 나는 나를 근근이 지키고 있다.

일상은 그 안에 비(非)일상을 품는다. 둘 사이의 긴장은 대치, 균형, 혹은 당착의 양상을 띤다. 현실은 외부의 실체이면서 생각과 감정이 유입되어 또 하나의 실체로 성장한다. 이렇게 일 플러스 일이 다시 일로 성장하는 순간을 언어의 두레박으로 품어내는 것이 시다.

"곤두선 고양이"가 "스치는 빛과 / 스미는 어둠의 대치" 속에 있다. 현실은 실루엣이 가장 짙어지는 다섯 시 반의 겨울 골목이다. 이 깔리는 어둠을 배경으로 석양은 "정점의 제련"에서 가장 예리하게 탄다. "불에 씻긴 불이 숨에 숨긴 숨을 / 오직 이글거리는 눈빛으로 맑게 내쉬는" 둥근 "홍반"은 현실 그 자체로 비현실을 녹여낸다. "겨울이 두 발로 서 있다." 현실과 비현실의 대치에서, 균형이든 당착이든, 겨울은 "골목에 깔리는 어둠의 무쇠 덫"과 "초공간의 문을 슬쩍 열어주는 석양의 닻" 양자에 묶여서 "당신이 보내는 연기 신호"를 찾고 있다(〈다섯 시 반의 덫은 나의 닻〉)

"운명의 지침"은 "길 위에" 서성이는 자가 "길 밖에" 떠 있는 것을 보는 자세에서 정해진다. 우리는 현실의 "접점을 따라 묵묵히" 걸으면서 여전히 딴 데를 "기웃거리고 있다." 현실에 짓눌리는 마지막 순간에서도 "광기의 미열이 다시 일어나기를" 고대하고 있다. "샘을 찾는다지만 / 심지어 샘을 판다지만 / 시가 시시콜콜 시답잖은 시간이" 세상을 지배한다. 그 길에서 우리는 길 밖의 "꽃짓이 오르락내리락 지휘하는 시월"의 가을을 바라본다. 강물이 말라서 바닥이 드러나기를 기다린다(〈강물이 말라야 강바닥이 드러나지〉).

현실의 수용은 어느 정도 체념의 미학에 의존한다. 그렇지만 정신은 이에 도전하여 반항적인 열망을 품는다. 새벽 한 시의 바닷가 천막에 앉아 빗소리를 듣는 사내가 있다. "두견새와 소쩍새 사이 어딘가에서" 울어대는 새 소리를 듣는다. 멀리 보이는 해안도로 가로등 불빛이 명멸한다. "삶의 테두리"는 "더러는 이빨 두셋 빠진 잇몸처럼 / 더러는 수명이 다해가는 손전등처럼 / 에둘러 명멸하는 한 가닥 영(零)의 행렬"로 세상을 에워싼다. 이 풍경을 조망하는 자는 몸과 마음이 밤의 혼돈을 향해 열린다. "우주의 광란"에 반응하는 자아는 "가부좌를 틀고 앉은 파락호"에서 "빗소리에 환생한 내장 없는 파라오"로 변신한다. 그렇다 해서 세상이 바뀌지는 않을 것이다. 자의식의 냉소에서 바람은 "식은 모주처럼 들쩍지근 깔리는 흰 라일락 향"을 풍기고 사라진다(〈자지 않는 새〉).

기교가 맛을 더한다: 유희

생각이 깊다고 해서 시가 위대해지지 않듯이 느낌이 강렬하다고 해서 감동을 주지는 않는다. 어디서나 구할 수 있는 소박한 재료인데도 누군가의 손맛에 이끌려 영혼을 깨우는 음식이 탄생한다. 시 또한 그러하다. 멋 부린 음식이 맛을 떨구듯이 기교가 넘친 시는 진정성을 잃는다. 그렇다고 무기교가 최상이지는 않다. 비유가 많다고 해서 나쁘지도 않고 적다고 해서 좋지도 않다. 적절하다는 것은 상대적이어서 그때마다 달라질 수 있다. 그런 가운데 화려하든 소박하든 언어를 능숙하게 다루는 기교와 재치는 감각을 일깨워 입맛을 돋운다. 시 쓰기는 주제와 소재에 앞서 언어를 요모조모 솜씨 있게 다루는 손맛을 요구한다.

가끔 "당신"으로 지칭하게 되는 반중력의 실체는 언어 그 자체일 수 있다. 직유나 은유는 유사성에 의존한다. 뜻하는 바를 직접 드러내지 않고 그를 대신해 줄 사물, 상황, 장면을 비유적으로 표현하는 일은 상상력을 요하고 그 과정이 시인과 독자 모두에게 발견과 몰입의 생동을 선사한다. 이와 대조적으로 환유는 유사성의 정도가 최소화된다. 원관념과 보조관념 사이의 유사성보다 그 차별성이 크게 드러난다. 시의 언어가 직유에서 은유로 다시 환유로 나아갈수록 원관념은 뒤에 감춰지고 보조관념이 전면에 대두된다.

나는 "갓 내린 커피 한 잔"이다. "당신"은 시집이다. 그런 당신에게 "뜨거운 환호"를 보내는 나만의 방식은 당신을 겹겹이 감추고 있는 시집에 와락 엎질러지는 것이다. 나의 "콩 볶은 탄내"가 당신의 "막장"까지 도달하는 동안 당신의 은유와 "온유한 환유"는 "폭발 직전의 응축이 안전밸브를 열고 / 간간이 내뱉던 물기둥"처럼 속뜻을 드러낼 것이다. 그리고 "바람의 저쪽으로 머쓱하게 흩어지는 / 그러다 허공으로 화하는 / 물 가루"로 사라질 것이다. 나도 당신도 시 속에 꼭꼭 숨어 있다. "자세를 유지하고 제때 물러서던" 당신이 속절없이 흔들려 폭발하듯이 나도 그러고 싶은지 모른다. 커피와 시집의 격한 포옹, 이렇게 "한동안 우리는 웅크릴 것이다"(〈당신이라는 환유〉)

사물은, 삶의 모든 세부는, 그 자체로 은유다. 상징인 듯 뜻을 은은히 내비치다가 어느새 사물로 돌아간다. 사물 그대로인데 어쩐지 그 물색이 바뀌고 다시 바뀐다. 사물과 사물이 무수히 몸을 바꾸는 황혼 무렵을 상징 체계로 통일하는 일은 덧없다. 그냥 다가오는 대로 품었다가 나가는 대로 놔두는 신의 한 수가 나의 기교면 좋겠다. 그런 때가 가끔 나를 덮친다. 나는 "광활한 너울이 모래 언덕 쪽으로 둥글게 넘어가는 저녁의 통(桶) 속에" 있다. 감각 안테나에 수신되는 수상한 파장에 반응하여 세상이 허물을 벗는다. 현실이 비현실적이어서 비현실이 현실적이다. "청색 소음이 분광(分光)에 일으키는 착란, 세상이 눌에서 셋으로 갈라지다가 분말로 번지기도" 한다. "사방에서 광대한 저녁이 무채색으로 압착"하는 공간에 소년이 서 있다. 그 자리 그대로 있으리라는 현실의 환상이 무너진다. 이럴 때, 누군가 "앞에서 간혹 대할 때보다 뒤에서 불현듯 안아줄 때," 길 위에서 길 밖의 당신을 느낄 때, 나는 "까마득히 가까운 운명"을 확인한다(〈반(半)-내림〉).

시의 언어는 유희의 언어다. 사물, 사건, 상황, 장면을 재현하는 과정에서 유희의 언어는 그 자체가 지닌 물성과 음악 그리고 동음이의 등의 요소로써 시인에게 만지작거리면서 놀이하는 손끝의 즐거움을 선사한다. 시인은 유희가 허용하는 자세에서 세상에 한결 초연해진 시선을 유지할 수 있다. 쓰디쓴 것이 달콤해지거나 심각한 것이 장난스러워지고 쏜살같이 사라지는 순간도 영원처럼 아른거릴 수 있다. 유희적 거리는 재현의 양상을 비틀어서 세상을 낯설게 하거나 개인적 경험을 보편적 예술 경험으로 확장하는 데 한몫을 담당한다.

새벽 꿈속에 찾아 헤매는 신이 한 켤레 신으로 드러나는 동음이의어 장난에서 "삶은 달걀"은 껍질이 벗겨지자 "둥근 달"로 뜨고 다시 그 자리에 "다행히 야한 흉터는 없으나 / 눈 코 입도 없"는 나신이 들어선다. 이러한 감각의 변덕은 "외로움이 그냥 달큼해지는 때"를 유희적으로 변주

한다(〈나의 신을 찾아서〉).

언어유희가 시에 풍미를 첨가한다. 흰 진눈깨비가 내리는 봄날의 저녁이다. 먼 하늘은 석양으로 물드는데 가깝고 낮은 하늘은 먹구름으로 덮여 있다. 아늑하게 기울어가는 빛을 배후에 두고 눈앞에 흩날리는 진눈깨비는 지상의 소용돌이를 타고 난무를 춘다. 세상이 비틀리면서 시간의 왜곡이 일어난다. 눈길에 미끄러져 추돌 사고가 일어나고 "누군가 무릎 꿇은 자세로 마룻바닥을 닦고 있다." 진눈깨비 틈새에서 장난 좋아하는 아기 도깨비가 놀고 있다. 여기저기 허공에 희끗거리는 자국이 모든 놓쳐버린 순간을 추모한다. 세상에 없고 그래서 사전에도 없을 "흰눈깨비"기 니에게 손짓한다 (〈흰눈깨비 날리는 저녁의 자태〉).

시선은 습관대로 먼 데로 향한다. 세상의 테두리는 그 너머와 이어져 있다. 지평선이 아니어도 수평선이 아니어도 시선의 끝에 사는 게 있다. 나에게서 가장 먼 내가, 당신이라고 불러야 마땅할 나 아닌 내가, 그곳에 산다. 그리하여 잊은 듯 지내던 "외면과 대면하는 국면이 오면" 나는 다가오지 않는 내가 그립다. 나 자신과 말장난을 한다. 유희의 언어는 시에 감미(甘味) 혹은 산미(酸味)를 첨가한다. 습관은 항체를 만든다. 부재 중인 자신을 대하는 일이 괴롭지만은 않다. 어쩌다 찾아올지도 모를 귀인 같아서 달콤하기까지 하다(〈내가 나를 보듬는 날〉).

민낯은 무정형이다: 형식

시는 장면마다 방백을 품는다. 난 무대에 홀로 서 있고 관객은 어둠 속에 있다. 혼자 속에서 그 속을 연출하듯 감독하듯 연기하듯 읊조린다. 관객은 없는 듯 있어서 난 무슨 짓을 하든 무한 자유롭되 그래도 혹 지켜보고 있을 누군가를 의식한다. 길 밖의 당신마저도 가끔 보이지 않는 관객이 된다. 내 말은 들어도 내게 말을 건네오지 않을 것을 알고 나는 당신에게 속정을 고백한다. 그래도 아무렇지 않으므로 당신은 거기 있고 나는 여기 있다. 이 역학은 왜 내 시의 골격을 이루는 것일까?

내가 붙잡을 수 없는 것이 있다. 하지만 그것은 언제든 나를 휘어잡을 수 있다. 그런 것에게는 "척, 악수를 청하는 게 상책이겠지요"(〈반내림〉). "날아가는 것은 뭐든 날아가게 두라"(〈흰눈깨비 날리는 저녁의 자태〉). "우리는 어찌 우러나는 것일까"(〈찻물 식어가는 소리〉). "전화해 볼까? / 아니"(〈세 시〉). "그냥 거기 있는 것만으로 / 충분히 여실한 / 넌 누구?"(〈다녀올게〉). "너희 씨족은 억새였을까"(〈금악행〉). 모두가 혼잣말이고 어둠 속의 독자에게 흘리는 방백이다.

간결하게, 뒤죽박죽 마구잡이로, 단선적으로, 공간적으로, 돌처럼 사물답게, 빛처럼 상징적으로, 난 이렇게 매 순간의 형식과 호흡을 찾으려 한다. 따라가는 데로 구해지는 데로 그 가치를 인정한다. 자유시는 정형성이 없다고 하나 그것은 시마다 고유의 정형이 있다는 뜻을 내포한다. 내 시의 무정형은 얼마나 정형에 도달하고 있을까? 문장이 길어지고 단어와 구문이 뱉어내듯이 던져지는 때가 있다. 이것을 간결하게 정제하는 것이 옳을까. 그럴 수 있고 그렇지 않을 수 있다. 때로 속에서 일어나는 혼탁한 물결을 거칠게 흘려보고 싶어진다. 이 순간의 매혹은 힘센 느낌의 추동에 있다. 사색의 정화가 형성하는 정적 응축 대신에 쏟아지고 분산하는 폭포의 힘줄이 결을 형성한다. 여러 이질적 장면과 동떨어진 시간이 뒤섞이는 듯해도 한결같은 사유적 감정의 분출이 줄기를 이룬다. 〈나는 날마다 가출한다〉, 〈반내림〉, 〈내가 나를 보듬는 날〉 등의 시에서 나는 자신을 내버려 두는 나를 본다. 이런 시가 어려운 듯해도 사실 쉽다면 쉽다. 굽이치는 강물이 그러하듯 자발적으로 그 형식을 갖추기 때문이다.

이에 반하여 짧은 시가 간결하고 투명한 듯해도 어려워지는 때가 종

종 있다. 더 응축되고 더 제련되며 더 다듬어지는 과정에서 더 감춰지고 더 확산하기 때문이다. 이 순간의 즐거움은 어깨에 힘이 빠지는 순간의 자유나 사유의 침잠에서 성취된다. 안으로 다시 그 안으로 가라앉으면서 시 쓰는 행위마저 무위의 몸짓으로 화하거나 간혹 평화로운 적요의 경험이 허용된다. 그럴 수 있고 그런 것이었으면 좋겠다. 〈목탁귀〉〈다섯 시반의 닻은 나의 닻〉〈산마루에 호수가 산다〉〈그라운드 제로〉 등의 시에서 나는 미니멀리스트의 언저리에 머문다. 다 비우지는 못했어도 그 가장자리에 서성이는 나를 본다.

맨 나중 독자에게 쓴다: 겨울

인생에서 "청춘에 모든 것을 걸고 / 기쁘게 무너질 수 있는" 누군가를 만난다면 어찌 기쁘지 않겠는가. "숨 한 결에 원고 한 매씩 낱낱이 읽혀" 깊이가 바닥까지 드러나고 "책 무덤"에 던져지더라도 스스로 무릎을 꿇을 수 있는 스승을 대할 수 있다면 어찌 즐겁지 않겠는가. 하지만 성장은 "몸짓과 말투마저 당신에게 맞춰온 / 아름다운 몽유(夢遊)의 시간"을 벗어나는 아픔을 요구한다. 들판의 "앉은뱅이 풀꽃"으로 살더라도 "홀로 피어날 용기와 자유"가 필요하다. 길 위에 있다. 가다 서다 하더라도 계속 간다. 당신의 품이 융숭하고 깊으나 그 "그림자의 낙원"은 나의 정처일 수 없다. 길은 "나 밖에 있는 당신 / 당신 밖에 있는 또 다른 당신" 너머로 끝없이 열려 있다(〈적에게〉).

나무 그늘에 앉는다. 나뭇잎이 햇살을 가려준다. 나무의 뒷모습에서 수천의 "지등(紙燈)"이 은은하게 켜지고 수천의 잎맥이 "당신의 담론을 이어간다." "스쳐서 번져오는 빛"이 고요를 감싸는 "그늘 한 칸"에 안겨 있다. 당신이 길가에 열어주는 그늘 속에 잠시 앉아 생각한다. 혼자 걸어온 길이 있을까? 길 가장자리 이 서늘한 은신처가 없다면 나는 어찌 여기까지 왔을까(〈그늘 한 칸의 골상학〉).

나를 위해 시를 쓴다. 나를 위한 것이기는 하나 나 자신을 노래한 적은 없다. 그렇다고 그냥 쓴다고 하기에는 그간에 쏟아낸 마음의 땀이 애처롭다. 아마도 나는 저 깊숙한 나에게 말을 건네온 듯하다. 첫 그리고 맨 나중 독자는 멀리 있는 나 자신인 것을 깨닫는다. 손에 잡힐 듯 잡히지 않는 "당신"조차도 여전히 내 안에 있다. 나는 "모래시계에 갇히는 때"가 있고 "구석진 곳 어딘들 박혀" 있으나 "감내할 수 없는 자전의 진동"으로 "어디론가 향하고 있다." "천년을 박혀" 있는 현실의 위압에서 "만년을 구른다"라는 "자전"의 의지는 결연하나 처연하다. 그것은 공염불의 목탁소리와 닮았다. 목탁의 두드림, 그 끝없는 출발은 지금쯤 어디에 도착하고 있을까. 유려하게 흘러가는 저 무염의 단조로운 파장이 수천의 시와 다르지 않다. 목탁이 내 안의 당신에게, 가장 멀리 있는 나 자신에게, 톡톡, 문을 두드리는 것, 이것이 나의 시일 것이다(〈목탁귀〉).

내 안에 잠들어 있는 맨 나중 독자를 향해, 여기, 내 방백의 속삭임을 흘려 쓴다.

흩날리는 진눈깨비의 오늘 아침처럼, 시간은 잿빛, 아니, 색을 잃은, 흩어지나 모여들고, 잡아끌어도 어렴풋할 따름인, 소환되어 해산되는

당신은 들숨을 쉬고 난 녹아든다

전방의 소수점들, 후방의 탄착점들

당신이 내게서 분해되어, 난 당신 안으로 사라진다

이제 만났고, 이제 헤어진다, 오전 8시, 나는 도시의 끝에 서 있고
당신은 들판의 시작에 누워 있다, 우린 어깨 나란히, 좋은 이웃일
뿐, 온 들판이 바람으로 채워지자 백색 소음이 물러간다

난 당신을 좋아하나, 당신은 나와 같지 않다

우리의 길이 언젠가 이어지기를!

우유, 커피?
블랙으로 주세요.

Epilogue: Apologia Pro Vita Mea et Poesi

I am not two; somehow, I am one. Like a flock of birds returning to the forest's edge at dusk, I come back, driven by a desire for unity. I am constantly tense, striving to be a single entity, just as you do. Reality exists. Whether I submit to it, ignore it, or mistakenly believe I have resisted it well, reality persists. And within it, there is me. I may be above or below, but I am always within it. Reality forms its own entity. There is no buffer zone between me and reality. Unless I am asleep, every direction is a battlefield. Perhaps, in my dreams, I fight even more fiercely.

Two ones, each maintaining their own substance, coexist. One against the other, and this coexistence is allowed only when neither is subordinate. Conflict arises from opposition: one tries to conquer the other.

For me, poetry is the trace of this neutral zone where two separate entities combine to once again become one. Poetry can be greater or smaller than reality. It can be higher or lower than I am. But in some way, poetry binds reality and me together as one. Even when this unity follows the logic of subtraction rather than addition, poetry transcends simple increase or decrease to form a new and different entity. This is why one minus one is not zero but, once again, one. I have never stepped outside reality. To me, poetry is always a new reality born from the constant tug-of-war between reality and myself, whether it unfolds "in a half-flat key" or "in a slightly sharp key."

I hope it stays that way.

Poetry Is Life: 1+1=1

Poetry does not originate solely from the head, nor does it stem purely from the heart. This series of negations suggests that poetry, in fact, emerges from all of these sources, as it requires the convergence of the poet's full capacity. Yet something essential is missing from these statements—an element crucial to the formation of poetry, though often overlooked. Perhaps it goes unnoticed because it seems so natural: poetry is the imagination of reality. In this idea, both imagination and reality hold equal weight. Poetry cannot arise without the workings of the mind, yet the mind reaches its greatest vitality through its close response to reality. So, what is this reality that stirs the mind and becomes indispensable to poetry?

The world itself is reality. But is it truly? The world exists as I see it, as I feel it, and as I think it. The world we perceive and express is the world we recognize through our senses, emotions, and thoughts. In a sense, the world is a construct, and the core components of this construct are both the world itself and the consciousness of the one perceiving it. In addition to these two primary elements, factors such as culture, tradition, ideology, and institutions shape the world. The more human intervention skews toward egocentrism, the more beautiful or ugly the world becomes; in extreme cases, the traces of the world itself may almost disappear. So, if the world is a construct, what is the best way to build it?

The world is reality, and poetry is imagination. This conventional dichotomy distorts the true nature of both poetry and the world. In this distortion, consciousness is removed from the world, and the world is excluded from poetry. In reality, the world reveals itself through consciousness, and the world is embedded within poetry as it is expressed. Both the world and poetry are shaped by the same principle: the fusion of consciousness and reality. As long as the world is a construct of the mind and poetry reflects that, they both embody this integration.

Imagination is a holistic mental capacity that respects the complexity of the world. When imagination engages with the specific details of life, the world reveals its full value. In the small, sheltered spaces where this interaction flourishes, the structure of the world becomes the structure of poetry. In a poetic village where reality manifests itself in both factual and non-factual ways, life is poetry and poetry is life.

Reality is like layered sediment, built up over time. At

its deepest level lie the quiet acceptance that "there are no flowers in the vase any longer" and the sense that countless noons or afternoons have become embedded with "the tiny swaying dots of baby's breath." On a day when "such fleeting moments pile softly on the bed," someone may hear "a metal spoon scraping on the bottom of an iron pot." This person is caught between "the vanished soul" and a day in which nothing unusual happens("I Run Away Every Day").

A day repeats itself, as "[m]y axis rotates horizontally," and life feels like "the very mire where I grow weary of another three-meal day"; at times, I feel the serene madness of "a suitably aged face, like your cool body"("When I Embrace Myself"). Daily life follows "the upright walk of the street trees, / [c]oming from where they come, going to where they go"("Journal of Ordinary Days"). The pavement reflects the true face of reality. Traffic lights guard safety, yet they "always change their face at zero." While the precast pavers in the sidewalk form a rhythmic foundation moving together in a continuous pattern, "corners live hidden in the seams," and as they "part, angles sharply form instantly"("Countdown").

Reality is subject to external forces beyond individual control. We live in a capitalist, liberally democratic country— the Republic of Korea. Between the characters of this sentence, historical, social, cultural, political, and economic events swirl. Even when we shut ourselves away, our windows and doors still face the public square. We may not always prioritize the contextual elements that shape reality, but we are inevitably exposed to and respond to them. We remember "the thirsty shouts she broadcast all over the Kwangju streets." From the memories of Kwangju in May 1980, it is clear that the value of what we enjoy today is the result of someone's sacrifice and bloodshed. Yet, the train moves forward, carrying those who have passed away, those who survived, and those living out their lives, with no pause in its course("When May Comes").

Why does history repeat its mistakes? What should never have happened arises from greed and keeps on occurring. Even today, somewhere in the world, there might be "the bus stop swallowed by the fallen apartment," "the journey home crushed in the back seat of the bus," and "the bridge swaying in the wind" falling into the Han river; and someone, somewhere, might open right now "the final message sent from beneath the blue water"("A Very Old Today"). Reality spreads over us precariously, like "a spray from the trail of the one going before / spatters on the window of the one following after"("Driving in the Rain").

The layers of reality, the closer they are to the surface, reveal more concrete and harder details of life. Every day presents the same scenes and events we confront morning and evening, neither mysterious nor beautiful. To avoid sinking beneath this surface, we need buoyancy. We must either look far ahead or breathe new life into the familiar. In the poem "Basil," "mom's lifetime and daughter's presence" form "two forces of reality I confront every day." In "You, Born in the Year of the Ox," reality is the unfamiliarity of a wife who has shared a life with the speaker for many years. "You," once thought to be fully known, once so familiar as to be forgotten, suddenly emerges as someone beyond any name the speaker can call. The wife transforms into "a daughter of a thousand years" who "[b]reak[s] free from the general frameworks of / 'Mother,' 'Darling,' 'Honey,' et cetera"("You, Born in the Year of the Ox"). Reality has a way of becoming more unfamiliar the more familiar it grows. It is a time and place where encounters and farewells repeat countless times. Perhaps for this reason, within the layers of long-standing reality, thousands of thoughts and feelings ripple like twilight after sunset, fading into abstract black and white as they drift toward the years gone by.

Two Paths Stretch, Side by Side, Separately: You

I am on a path, but there is also a path outside this path, at the margins of life, where those antigravitational beings exist— referred to as you, thee, and thou. Like anyone else, I follow the course of life. Along this course, I walk with those who seem to lead or follow me, whether far or near. Yet, even as we walk side by side, we are not on the same path. An untraveled road runs parallel to my life's journey. Walking back and forth along this boundary, we have become companions, almost without noticing. Reality and unreality brush against each other, resembling one another. Reality sustains its aspirations through unreality, while unreality finds its footing in reality. The fusion of the real and the unreal creates another reality—a realm that poetry seeks to manifest. One plus one becomes one again. In this way, reality becomes imaginative, and imagination gets real.

"You" is a poetry collection intricately woven with metonymies and metaphors, distilling the essence of a life into its purest form. The speaker, yearning to draw closer—or perhaps to be embraced by this life—spills over the pages like a cup of hot coffee, saturating and transforming the collection. In this process, the work twists and contorts into "a certain twisted volcanic terrain," as if bracing for the eruption of a geyser. Just as metaphor and metonymy embody ambiguity, so too does the figure of "you," holding life's complexities within gestures where "the contact points of relationships, refined and blurred," slip elusively from view. The speaker longs to crouch beside "you," sharing in this distilled intimacy. Perhaps this "you" is none other than the speaker themselves—or the poetic world meticulously crafted by the poet. "You, who maintained posture and withdrew at the right time," may, in fact, be the speaker's own silhouette, "[s]catter[ing] awkwardly to the other side of the wind"("You, Whom I Call Metonymy").

"You" may refer to the act of writing poetry itself. The chronic signs of habitual writing become evident in the moment when "[w]hite rust forms on the tip of a neglected pen," and the speaker finds themselves trapped in "the eternal self-cloning." Here, the speaker acknowledges the discomfort of writing, recognizing "I am always a blind spot, starting from you as the origin." Poetry longs for the "you" who exists outside the path, while I remain on the path. "You" constantly calls out, awakening and beckoning, but I can never quite reach. We move forward together, yet the distance between us never closes enough("Long-Standing Words on Earth").

There are moments when I feel unable to escape the grip of something profound. Sometimes, it is the weight of life pressing down on my soul; other times, it is the antigravity that lifts me, helping me resist that burden. Reality is hard to elude, and even harder to overcome. Writing poetry becomes an attempt to confront or find balance within this reality. Poetry rides a seesaw between "the noises of the world" and the "deep blue depth" that stretches toward "whatever resides in the distance." The rhythmic flow of emotions and thoughts—origin of most of my poetry—follows this dynamic. "[T]hat companion / [s]urging inside, poking and aching, / [a]fter denying me long-awaited expectations," or "[t]hat elusive figure, / [b]arely visible, always trailing behind / [o]n the backward path of my life" is the occasional guardian whose presence brings poetry to me. I have, at times, been a master of resignation, accepting "the wind's empty hands"; then a seeker, casting my transcendent gaze far beyond, only to return to the world as a realist, indulging in "four-pronged cucumber pickles." The pulse of writing poetry aligns with the rhythm that drives life. Since I cannot escape this throbbing flow, writing poetry is my destiny, my companion at the edge of life's winding road("Companion").

"You" may also refer to moments of solitude when one confronts oneself. What the inward glancing brings up, in the time of being alone, becomes an object for observation and contemplation. The "dizziness from paths not taken," which has accompanied me throughout my life, is qualified as "you," a persona of companionship("Lonely"). In the noisy corner of a café, as dusk approaches, the heart's door opens to a far distant field—into "a small god's space," where isolation becomes endurable. It is here that I reach myself, "[w]ith my ears open in four directions." In such a moment, whoever meets "you" just outside the path will prick their ears and listen("The Afternoon Pan").

I Move Forward While Stumbling Backward: Posture

Even though life may seem like a series of missteps, time steadily finds its own direction. At times, one responds to a deep, almost hidden calling, whether from the body or the mind. These moments, initially sporadic, eventually cling like shadows, and I see a path gradually becoming clear. I have both struggled against it and lived in alignment with it. There are mistakes I repeat over and over; in the paradoxical acceptance that these errors shape who I am, I find myself on my own path. Perhaps it is the desire to foresee, even to predetermine, the vague, flickering fate that often urges certain postures and far-reaching aims to appear in my poetry.

The contact points of my soles shape the path I walk. Poetry begins along the edges of the path where I fix my gaze. There is a destination, near yet untouchable, distant yet ever-present. I will face the day when "whatever can summon youth is lost," in the presence of absence or the absence of presence. When that day comes, "[t]he origin of species" will be forgotten, "[e]ven [my] name erased," like "hollow culms, purer than anything in this world." Standing before a stretch of dry grass brushing the windy ridge, I watch "steel brooms" sweeping the wind's path and "a bright wave of whipping rods" rising above me. These rods, with their bright strokes, teach me to hold my posture to the very end, to keep the windy west as "guardian of the sunset's contour"("Journey to Geumak, the Volcanic Cone").

Someone, gazing along the path, yearns to feel the wind with "its indifferent mind" as it "[s]oftly pass[es] through the zelkova leaves' / [t]housands of silent vibrations"("Such a White

Herd of Cattle"). Swayed by the view from a bus window, this figure longs to be "a boy with his legs bare" once more, to "[w]alk haughtily into the silver flood"("Into the Silver-White Sands"). Upon reaching the mountain's summit, one might wonder, "I wonder if I should at least delay the descent / [t]o erase my own name"("Delay the Descent"). Standing before the mirror at the hairdresser's, I imagine shaving my head like "a monk on a dark moon night," hoping to rid myself of "this nameless grass regrowing / [a]s it pleases"("Nameless Grass").

The posture of soothing and gathering oneself often intertwines with that of negation and emptying. The seeker on the path seeks to embody "my lithe form slowly fading away, / [j]ust before a sudden shower pours down"("When It's Cloudy and Windy"). My gaze rests not on vertical heights but on the equality of the horizon. Yet, I also strive to walk upright: "I rise on tiptoe, straining to see farther, / [s]tanding as best I can, as needed." Observing "the grass's electrocardiogram" etched flat at ground zero, I adopt a posture of reflection. My bipedal stance, "holding steady in the heart of the moment," confronts trauma along "a six-mile stretch of sprawling fields." Between the ever-tense self and the field "lying straight beneath the sky," the seeker seems to yearn for rest("Ground Zero").

Reflecting on moments when I insisted on my opinions to a junior while "feigning incompetence to a senior," I survey the path I have walked("I Again Talked Too Much Yesterday").

Though I traverse the contact points of my feet, I cultivate a pensive mind, "[w]ith eyelids horizontally closed / [a]nd Buddha's ears vertically open," embracing the emptiness that transcends distraction("Companion").

Affection Bears the Color of Yeast: Love

There are moments when I suddenly realize I may still be a naive romantic. Like rice wine that clouds when shaken, then slowly clears into a soft, translucent, yeast-like glow, so does affection mature. The chaos of reality filters through the sieve of time, fermenting and distilling into a small measure of essence—not yet wholly pure. This is love, and in this way, it becomes poetry.

Memory is "the tea water cooling blandly, / [a]fter boiling, swirling, steeping, and settling." It is peaceful to start a day with tea in the "morning yard, / [w]here nothing has yet unfolded after its tidy-up." In the teacup, "the secret sourness of hidden love" dissolves, and "the bright yellow of hillside sunlight / [e]xtracted by early-May leaves" blends. If only the tangled threads of time could unwind in such a way("The Sound of Tea Cooling").

Time doesn't always move forward, just as people don't always live entirely separate lives. Within your face lives someone "[w]ho cared about you more than you do yourself."

"my mother-in-law's gray hair" grows "[a]round my wife's ear, buried in the sofa"("When I Burn Incense with the Door Open"). Along the margins of time's current, where "[a] summer spills over into another summer, / [o]verflowing again recklessly into numerous summers," there arrives a morning when "sunlight fully surrounds her," and an evening falls when "shadows stand guard around her"("In a Slightly Sharp Key"). In memories, "[i]n a pot sour with age," sometimes "an alcoholic flower" emerges, and a boy within me sits on the steps of PO Cafe, singing "The River of No Return"("Hoo-Hoo").

Though family is a poetic subject prone to sentimentality, it opens an effective gateway for the realist's aesthetic exploration. Family is the poetic reality where joy, anger, sorrow, and pleasure mature. Few entryways offer a better glimpse into another world than through this door. In the poem "Largo in a Cup of Coffee and an Apple," love is defined as "finding two apples / [i]n a kimchi refrigerator reeking of musty days." But love also includes placing those apples "separately on two plates," then "taking out the yellow-handled knife / [h]idden in a messy drawer and sharpening its blade." Love is not born of romance, but rather from conflict and reconciliation. Even in peeling apples, there are two methods: one involves cutting them into six slices before peeling, the other peeling them whole while turning them around. Love is not a blazing flame, but rather "rearranging those bare pieces, / [h]earing them confess their cold, dense solidity, one by one"—a process of dialogue and compromise. Reality is neither hell nor heaven. It is not purgatory either, so while heaven feels distant, hell can loom close. Love and poetry are the forces that allow us to accept life on earth and, within it, to whisper briefly to ourselves, "This is beautiful."

Thoughts and emotions ferment; what ripens gives form to abstraction. This is an aspect of reality. One plus one or one minus one becoming one again—that's how life unfolds. Poetry arises from life. Whatever enters and exits the body and mind leaves traces, yet the accumulation of those traces is not solid. Sometimes, they're washed away by rain. Angles and edges wear down and erode, gathering as silt along the riverbank of time, completing the equation of resonance. On the brink of life dwell things that are neither mere thoughts and emotions nor simply things. The body and mind are places where resonance vibrates. A collection of poems is, perhaps, a house of resonance tracing the edges of such a life.

Ordinary Is Metaphysical,
and Metaphysical Ordinary: Poetics

Romanticism and idealism lack the strength to confront reality—this is the thought I softly murmur to the wall. A counter-reality must possess the tangible force of reality itself.

Shouldn't a poet seek strength within reality to stand against it? Anti-gravity is not the absence of gravity but a force that defies it. Similarly, the freedom poetry seeks is not transcendence but a state where oppressive weight is weakened or neutralized. Grounded on earth, the poet relies not on God but on the mind—without succumbing to egotism—respecting reality while refusing to be crushed by its weight. This mind, imbued with the force of anti-gravity, neither distorts nor romanticizes reality. How can such a mind manifest in poetry? How does the reality it perceives, constructs, and represents unfold in both life and poetry?

The vitality of the mind—this is our ultimate refuge. But how can the mind be fully activated to reach its utmost potential? T.S. Eliot criticized the "dissociation of sensibility" in earlier eras, calling for the reintegration of thought and feeling. Historically, mental activity has oscillated between the poles of emotional power and intellectual rigor. Like oil and water, thought and emotion resist easy blending. When rational thought seeks universal values, it often suppresses personal emotions and individuality. Conversely, emotion, while transcending logic and facts to enrich and deepen our perception of the world, risks losing objectivity in the process. Following the rationality of the 18th century, the imagination of the 19th, and the 20th century's efforts to integrate sensibility, what new pathways does writing in the 21st century offer? How might we harmonize the mind's intellectual and emotional capacities to craft a more unified and potent understanding of the human experience?

In a world where absolutes have vanished, achieving harmony while respecting individual differences requires a profound commitment to objectivity. The world reveals itself only through consciousness. How, then, does the mind—through its intricate workings—shape our awareness of reality? How can thought and feeling operate in tandem, each maintaining its distinct value while compensating for the other's limitations? Most critically, how can this delicate and expansive interplay find its ultimate expression in poetry?

In his "Preface" to *Lyrical Ballads* (1800), William Wordsworth offers a profound perspective on the interplay between thought and feeling, challenging their conventional dichotomy. He famously describes great poetry as "the spontaneous overflow of powerful feelings." Yet, these feelings are not unrefined; they are shaped through reflection, as "our continued influxes of feeling are modified and directed by our thoughts." Moreover, thoughts themselves serve as "representatives of all our past feelings." By examining the interaction of these "general representatives," Wordsworth suggests we can uncover what is truly essential in life. For Wordsworth, the poet becomes a mediator, contemplating these "representatives of feelings" to reveal "what is really important to men" and sustaining this cycle of discovery. In this process of "organic sensibility," thought and feeling are inextricably intertwined, continuously shaping and elevating one another in a dynamic, symbiotic relationship.

How, then, can thought and feeling truly unite? Wordsworth's concept of "organic sensibility" and Eliot's notion of sensibility share similarities yet diverge in emphasis. For Eliot, the dissociation and subsequent reintegration of sensibility represent a historical shift in how thought and feeling are perceived and expressed. In contrast, Wordsworth views this interplay as a deeply personal process at the heart of creativity. Wordsworth's poetry often adopts a didactic tone, as his emotions are carefully filtered through an individualistic and idealistic lens. Enriched by reflection, his work is suffused with imagery of idyllic nature, harmonizing emotional depth with contemplative resonance. Eliot, on the other hand, envisions a sensibility cultivated unconsciously through the integration of life's complexities—historical, cultural, and personal dimensions—yielding a deeper and more collective resonance.

Wordsworth's concept of "organic sensibility" is deeply rooted in the Romantic tradition, relying on personal reflection to elevate emotions to the sublime. In contrast, Eliot's sensibility embraces a modernist framework, rejecting excessive subjectivity in favor of what he terms the "historical sense." For Wordsworth, emotions attain transcendence through individual and introspective contemplation, often drawn from nature and personal experience. Eliot, however, advocates for an impersonal approach, where emotions are not directly expressed but conveyed indirectly through the use of "objective correlatives"—a set of objects, situations, or events designed to evoke specific emotions in the reader.

William Carlos Williams' imagism exemplifies intellectual precision, rejecting what Ezra Pound derided as the "emotional slither" characteristic of Romanticism. By presenting solid objects as they are, Williams resists emotional indulgence and the self-centered imposition of meaning, granting objects a freedom independent of human dominance. His dictum, "no ideas but in things," underscores a deliberate engagement with the world's inherent beauty, emphasizing the tangible and the particular. Williams sought to liberate objects from conceptual dominance by focusing on parts rather than wholes and on discontinuous moments rather than the continuity of time. For him, the poet's mind reaches its fullest potential not by imposing unity or seeking "a common relationship," but by discerning "in things those inimitable particles of dissimilarity to all other things."

The mind draws its vitality from integrated sensibility—a concept whose importance is easy to emphasize but difficult to define in terms of its realization. Major poets in the English and American traditions have approached this integration in diverse ways. How, then, should a poet's mind function in our time to effectively engage with reality? For instance, 21st-century poet Jorie Graham dramatizes the tension between immediate response and conscious skepticism. In her poetry, sensitive perceptions remain open, while thought resists confinement to any fleeting conclusion. Her work deconstructs and rebuilds itself, perpetually moving toward new realizations. This seemingly negative, questioning spirit becomes inherently constructive, as reality dissolves into illusion and illusion back into reality, creating fresh foundations for an ever-unfinished process of awakening.

My poetic tastes and temperament have been profoundly shaped by the rich and expansive canon of English and American poetry. Writing with precision and rigor became second nature as I immersed myself in the dense forest of English and American criticism. From my first collection to the present, my poetry reflects gestures influenced by these traditions while retaining my own distinct temperament. For me, the act of writing poetry is a direct confrontation with reality. Poets such as Wordsworth, Eliot, Williams, and Graham each embody a unique form of anti-gravity, transcending the weight of existence in their distinct ways. Within this delicate balance, the particulars of life occasionally radiate a metaphysical glow. The ordinary transforms into the metaphysical, and the metaphysical dissolves into the ordinary—a poetic proposition that continues to guide and inspire me.

In poetry, emotions are modified and directed by thoughts. At the intersection where thoughts and feelings converge, the everyday transforms into the metaphysical, and the metaphysical becomes ordinary. A potted plant by the window, for instance, reveals this interplay: "the flower opened its white lapels wide," evoking for the speaker "a slightly flirtatious woman." Over time, this relationship evolves "from dislike to fondness, from disdain to indifference," until the speaker quietly concludes, "[w]e're just friends." Yet, after years of blooming, this friend shows "no sign of flowers" all spring. Standing beside such a companion, the speaker softly murmurs, "Please, just don't get sick"("Jasmine").

Solitude is an integral part of daily life, intricately woven into the fabric of reality. Inescapable, it lingers until we internalize it as part of ourselves. Like breath, solitude quietly inhabits the world, moving as an unseen spirit, "flowing through the veins of all things / [f]eeding off life everywhere." Objects bear solitude, and loneliness emerges as a fundamental condition of existence, embedding itself in the world like "the twisted mind of a parasitic brother"("Lonely"). For me, lyricism becomes an object of scrutiny, often accompanied by a self-mocking awareness. Even as lyricism pours forth, it is observed in its unfolding, becoming both expression and reflection. A poet does not merely articulate loneliness but engages in thoughtful observation, unraveling its essence.

Flowers bloom from grasses, their identity shaped by perspective—whether regarded as flower or grass. Perhaps maturity is the transformation of grass into flower. In June, I lose myself in the trumpet calls of lilies. Flowers gather, becoming "stepping stones for us to cross the oak tree's domain." As "hearts revealed through bodies," they embody "the sound and fury of the path to midsummer," arriving in the world as "[t]he daughters of the earth," each with its own purpose. A "three-leaf flower" might signify purity, yet we may "forget the language of flowers entirely," reducing it to "[n]othing more than a wooden sign / [p]lanted in the flower bed of an abandoned school." It is June. Today is simply today. "Dance to the music stored in these trumpets"("Soliloquy on Floriography").

Poetry is inherently lyrical. Yet, perhaps due to prolonged exposure to lyricism or the development of an antibody to its familiar forms, I no longer find freshness in lyricism itself but in reflecting on it and probing its nuances. In a world saturated with proclaimed truths, I often resist these self-evident revelations. Rather than accepting truth as a given, I find deeper awakenings in its absence, its negation, or in the rhythm of self and language striving toward it. Lyricism, then, becomes a meditation on itself, and truth transforms into a journey rather than a fixed destination. This is the essence I seek in my poetry today.

Life Is Conflict or Contradiction: Balance

To me, poetry aligns with Wallace Stevens' definition: it is "a particular of life thought about for so long that one's thought becomes an inseparable part of it, or a particular of life so intensely felt that the feeling enters into it." This perspective does not assign poetry a distinct theoretical domain but instead embraces its capacity to capture the reality unfolding around us. The world, as Stevens describes, is "a compact of real things so like the unreal things of the imagination that they are indistinguishable from one another." His insight—that these details of reality are "a part of our vital experience of life"— forms the foundation of my own modest poetics.

New excitements have emerged as I begin to perceive the world in ways previously unfamiliar to me. These changes are not born of writing techniques or linguistic ingenuity but from an evolving awareness and attitude toward life. Reality cannot be ignored, blindly accepted, or transcended; life is a constant negotiation between ideals and the real. Human affairs consist of layers of light and shadow, forming endless abstractions shaped by how they are stirred. Romanticism, ideals, and notions sometimes exist beyond reality and, at other times, within it. How they integrate into reality—through compromise, mediation, or balance—differs in every instance.

A poet's individuality and originality arise from their ability to sense and pursue this delicate process of reconciliation.

In my poetry, the cup cradling the sound of cooling tea, the jasmine by the living room window, the upside-down yogurt bottle on the table near the refrigerator, and the field at dusk in "in a half-flat key" have all been inhabited by thoughts and emotions for so long that they have become inseparable from them. They exist as both reality and unreality. In this space, where life transforms into poetic terrain, I barely manage to hold onto myself.

The everyday holds the extraordinary within itself. The tension between the two emerges as opposition, balance, or contradiction. Reality, as an external entity, transforms into another form of reality when infused with thought and emotion. Poetry is the art of capturing this moment—when one plus one becomes one again—using language as its vessel.

A "bristling cat" stands "[b]etween the passing light and the seeping darkness." Reality unfolds in the winter alley at 5:30 p.m., where silhouettes reach their darkest. Against the encroaching dusk, the sunset blazes "[a]t the precise peak of smelting," and the "round rash," revealed as "[f]ire bathed in fire, breath hidden in breath, / [r]eleased only through a gaze ablaze," becomes the threshold where reality merges into unreality. "Winter stands on two feet." In the interplay of reality and unreality—whether balanced or contradictory—winter seeks "the smoke signal you send," tethered to both extremes: "[t]he iron-dark trap set in the alley, / [a]nd the anchor of the sunset, / [g]ently prying open the door to hyperspace"("The 5:30 Trap Is My Anchor").

"This, I decree as fate" is declared by one who, lingering on the path, gazes beyond it. We walk silently "along the meeting points of our soles," yet our glances continually seek something beyond. Even in our final moments, crushed by reality, we "wish for the fever of madness to stir again in [us]." We are said to search for a spring, even vowing that "we will dig one," yet "time, so petty in every detail," governs the world. On that path, we look toward autumn, where "[d]ozens of flowers wavering in the air, / [s]ubmitting to the wind, / [b]ending and straightening, / [l]owering and rising," conduct October's rhythm with their gestures. We wait for the river to dry up, so that "[t]he riverbed is revealed"("The Riverbed Is Revealed Only When the River Dries Up").

Accepting reality leans into the aesthetics of resignation, yet the spirit resists, harboring defiant aspirations. At one a.m., a man sits under a tent on a seaside hill, listening to the sound of rain. A bird's cry drifts somewhere "between the cuckoo and the scops owl." In the distance, street lamps along the coastline flicker. "The edge of life" encircles the world, marked by "[a] procession of zeros, flickering and fading"—"[s]ometimes like a gum with a few missing teeth, /

[s]ometimes like a flashlight, nearing the end of its battery." The observer opens both body and mind to the chaos of the night. Responding to the "cosmic turmoil," the self transforms— "once a rogue, sitting cross-legged in a lotus position, / [t]hen a Pharaoh, emptied of his insides, reincarnated by the sound of rain." Yet, this transformation holds no promise that the world itself will change. From the cynicism of self-awareness, the wind carries away "the scent of white lilacs," lingering "like raw rice wine cooling off"("A Sleepless Bird").

Technique Adds Flavor: Play

Just as deep thoughts alone don't automatically make a poem great, powerful emotions don't always guarantee impact. A dish with soul-stirring flavors can emerge from simple ingredients when prepared with a special touch. Poetry is much the same. Overly elaborate dishes risk losing their essence, just as a poem overloaded with technique can lose its sincerity. Yet this doesn't mean that a lack of technique is ideal. A poem isn't inherently weaker for having too many metaphors, nor stronger for having too few. What's appropriate is always relative, shifting with each occasion. Whether lavish or simple, skillful use of language through technique and wit awakens the senses and sharpens the appetite. Writing poetry requires a deft touch with language, an ability to balance its weight and texture, regardless of theme or subject.

At times, the "you" addressed in my poetry may be language itself, embodying a kind of anti-gravity. Similes and metaphors depend on similarity, inviting meaning to emerge indirectly through objects, situations, or scenes rendered figuratively. This imaginative process provides both poet and reader with a dynamic experience of discovery and immersion. By contrast, metonymy minimizes similarity, drawing sharper distinctions between the original idea and its substitute. As poetic language evolves from simile to metaphor and eventually to metonymy, the original concept recedes into the background, while its substitute takes center stage.

I am "a freshly brewed cup of coffee." You are a poetry collection. My way of sending you "[h]ot cheers" is to spill myself across the layers of poems that conceal you. As "the smell of roasted beans" seeps into your "abysmal depths," your metaphors and "gentle metonymy" unveil their deeper meanings, like "a column of water, sporadically exhaling / [as] the safety valve opens just before the explosion." Then, they vanish, "[s]catter awkwardly to the other side of the wind / [a]nd dissolve into the void." Both you and I are deeply hidden within the poetry. Just as "you, who maintained posture and withdrew at the right time," might suddenly falter and erupt, perhaps I, too, long for the same. The intense embrace of coffee and a poetry collection—"[f]or a while, we will crouch"("You, Whom

I Call Metonymy").

Objects, and all the details of life, are metaphors in themselves. They subtly hint at symbolic meanings, only to return to being mere objects once more. There they are, yet ever-shifting, their colors transforming again and again. Attempting to unify the endless metamorphoses of twilight objects into a single symbolic system is futile. My craft, I hope, resembles a masterstroke—embracing things as they come and letting them go as they leave. I am sometimes overtaken by moments like this. I find myself "in the vast barrel of evening, which swells and rolls toward the sand dunes." Responding to strange signals picked up by my sensory antennae, the world begins to shed its layers. Reality becomes unreal, and the unreal turns real. "The confusion caused by blue noise splits the spectrum, dividing the world from two into three, sometimes scattering it into powder." A boy stands in a space where "the vast hollow of evening compresses into monochrome," and the illusion of a reality standing still forever crumbles. In such moments, when "embraced from behind rather than when occasionally facing you," sensing "you" beyond the path, I confirm "the proximity of distant fate"("In a Half-Flat Key").

The language of poetry is a language of play. As objects, events, situations, and scenes are represented, the playful qualities of language—its texture, rhythm, music, and homophones—offer the poet the joy of handling it as if their fingers were at play. Through this playful stance, the poet gains a detached, serene perspective on the world. Bitterness can turn sweet, seriousness can become lighthearted, and fleeting moments can shimmer as though eternal. This playful distance distorts modes of representation, defamiliarizing the world and transforming personal experiences into universal artistic expressions.

In the playful pun of homophones, the soul I seek in my early morning dreams reveals itself as a pair of soles. Through this wordplay, "a boiled egg," once peeled, becomes "an oval moon," where "[t]hankfully, there are no obscene scars, / [nor are there eyes, a nose, or a mouth." These whimsical transformations mirror the quiet realization that "[l]oneliness is sometimes simply sweet"("Finding My Shoes").

Wordplay brings an added richness to poetry, infusing it with unexpected flavors. It's a spring evening, and white sleet is falling. The distant sky is tinged with the hues of sunset, while the nearby sky darkens beneath heavy clouds. Against the backdrop of warm, slanting light, the swirling sleet before my eyes dances in the wind's whirl. As the world tilts, time seems to distort. A car collides with another on the icy road, and "[s]omeone scrubs the floor, down on her knees." Amid the falling sleet, a mischievous hobgoblin child plays. White flecks shimmer in the air, commemorating moments irretrievably lost to time. The "white hobgoblin sleet"—a thing that exists neither in reality nor in any dictionary—beckons to me, inviting me to step into its fleeting, enchanted world("The Figure of an Evening When White Hobgoblin Sleet Drifts Down").

My gaze habitually turns toward the distance. The edge of the world connects to what lies beyond. Even when it isn't the horizon or the skyline, something always exists at the end of my gaze. The farthest version of myself—the one who should rightly be called "you"—dwells there. So, when I confront "a face that turns from what I've faced," I yearn for the part of myself that never draws closer. I engage in wordplay with myself, weaving playful language that adds sweetness or tartness to poetry. Habit fosters immunity. Facing my absent self is not entirely painful—there's even a certain sweetness to it, as though it were a noble soul destined to visit me one day("When I Embrace Myself").

Bare Face Is Amorphous: Form

Almost every scene in my poetry carries the air of a soliloquy or an aside. Alone on stage, I stand with the audience shrouded in darkness. Directing, producing, and performing all at once, I murmur into the solitude. Though the silent audience grants me the freedom to express myself, I remain keenly aware that someone may still be watching. Even you, beyond the path, sometimes become part of this unseen audience. I know you hear me, though you never respond, and so I confess my innermost feelings. Yet, nothing feels strange—there you are, and here I am. Why does this dynamic shape the very structure of my poetry?

There are things I cannot grasp, yet they seize hold of me. With such things, "it's best to shake hands with what holds me"("In a Half-Flat Key"). "Let whatever flies, fly"("The Figure of an Evening When White Hobgoblin Sleet Drifts Down"). "How do we steep ourselves?"("The Sound of Tea Cooling"). "Should I make a call? / No"("At Three O'Clock"). "Just your being here / [m]akes my time strikingly vivid. / Who are you?"("I'll Be Back"). "Were your ancestors silver grass?"("Journey to Geumak, the Volcanic Cone"). Each line becomes a soliloquy or an aside, whispered to the unseen reader in the dark.

Simply, haphazardly, whether in a linear or spatial way, as solid as stone or as symbolic as light, I constantly seek the form and rhythm of each moment, following wherever it leads and recognizing its value as it unfolds. While free verse may seem formless, each poem discovers its own distinct structure. How close does the amorphousness of my poetry come to achieving its unique form? Sometimes, sentences stretch long, words and phrases cast out as if spat. Should I refine them into something more concise? Perhaps. Perhaps not. At times, I feel compelled to let the turbulent waves within flow roughly. The allure lies in the raw force of emotion—not the static condensation shaped by careful reflection, but the dispersing energy, like threads of a waterfall creating texture. Even when various scenes and fragmented times seem to blur together, the continuous surge of reflective emotion forms the core. In poems like "I Run Away Every Day," "In a Half-Flat Key," and "When I Embrace Myself," I witness a self letting go. Though these poems may seem complex, they are, at heart, simple—shaping themselves spontaneously, like a river winding its own course.

In contrast, short poems, though concise and transparent, often prove more challenging. As they condense, refine, and polish, they conceal as much as they reveal. The joy of these moments lies in releasing tension or immersing deeply in contemplation. As everything turns inward, even the act of writing becomes a gesture of non-action, allowing a serene void to emerge. This approach feels both possible and desirable. In poems like "An Ear to Moktak's Knocking," "The 5:30 Trap Is My Anchor," "A Lake Nestles on the Mountain Crest," and "Ground Zero," I find myself hovering on the edge of minimalism. Though I have not completely emptied everything, I sense myself wandering along its boundaries.

I Write to the Last Audience: Winter

To meet someone in life to whom "I could surrender myself joyfully," wagering everything on my youth—how could that not bring joy? Even if "[m]y manuscripts, / read upon your folded knees, one page per breath, / then discarded into the grave of books," revealed the shallowness of my soul, it would still be a delight to encounter a mentor before whom I could willingly kneel. Yet, maturing demands the painful shedding of "those beautiful, dreamlike days / when I aligned even my gestures and voice with yours." Even if I live "as a weed, / growing tall, feathered leaves, speckled with dirt," I need "the courage and freedom to bloom alone." I am on the path. Even if I stop and start again, I keep moving. As generous and deep as your embrace may be, that "paradise of shadows" cannot be my final destination. The path stretches endlessly, "to you outside me, / and to the you beyond you"("To My Enemy, 2004").

I sit beneath a tree, its leaves shielding me from the burning sun. Behind it, thousands of "paper lanterns" glow faintly, and thousands of leaf veins "[c]ontinue your eloquent discourse." Enveloped in "[l]ight, seeping and submerging," I pause for a moment in the tranquil shade you cast by the roadside, reflecting, "Have I truly walked this path alone?" Without this cool refuge at the edge, how could I have come this far?("Phrenology of a Shaded Haven, 2024").

I write poems for myself. Though they are meant for me, I have never celebrated myself. Yet to say I simply write would diminish the emotional sweat I have poured into them. Perhaps I have been speaking to the deepest part of myself all along. I now realize that my first and final reader is the distant version of me. Even the elusive "you" still resides within. There are moments when I find myself "caught in an hourglass" or "wedged in some secluded corner," yet I move forward, driven by the "unbearable vibration of self-rotation." The will to "[roll] for ten thousand," while "[e]mbedded for a thousand years," is both resolute and poignant. It calls to mind the rhythmic tapping of a moktak—the steady, endless sound. Where might its persistent rapping, its never-ending beginnings, have arrived by now? That immaculate wave, flowing smoothly in its monotony, mirrors thousands of poems. The moktak's knocking echoes at the door of "you," the version of myself farthest away. This is how my poetry must be("An Ear to Moktak's Knocking").

Here, I scribble my whispered asides, reaching for the final audience, still dormant within me.

Like this morning's fluttering sleet, time feels ashen—or perhaps it has lost all color. It drifts apart only to gather again, elusive as I try to grasp it, summoned only to scatter.

You inhale, and I dissolve.

Decimal points ahead, bullet points behind.

You fall away from me, and I disappear into you.

Now we meet, now we part. It's 8 a.m. I'm standing at the edge of the city, and you lie at the beginning of the landscape. Side by side, we are merely good neighbors. As the wind courses through the fields, the white noise fades away.

I like you, but you are unlike me.

May our paths converge one day.

Milk or coffee?
Black, please.

작가 노트

한영상성시집(韓英相成詩集)은 지구촌 독자를 향해 한국의 시를 영시의 형식으로 재창조하고 두 판본을 나란히 제시하면서 시인의 시론 혹은 비평가의 평설을 함께 싣고자 한다. 두 가지 시 형식의 병존은 문화의 차이와 닮음을 선명하게 드러내고 번역의 노역에도 불가피하게 초래되는 손실을 가시화함으로써 역설적으로 서로를 보완하고 시의 이해를 완수하는 데 보탬을 줄 것이다.

목탁은 불교 의식에 필수적인 한국 전통 타악기이다. 손에 들고 사용하는 이 나무로 만든 악기는 보통 물고기 모양을 하고 있으며, 타격 시 맑고 울림 있는 소리를 낸다. 목탁은 독경과 의식 중 리듬을 유지하고 템포를 조율하며 집중을 돕는 데 사용된다. 그 일정하고 명상적인 음색은 불교 수행에서 없어서는 안 될 도구이다.

Author's Notes

The Korean-English Symbiotic Poetry Series seeks to reimagine Korean poetry in English for a global audience, presenting the original alongside its translation, complemented by the poet's reflections or a critical essay. This coexistence of two poetic forms highlights both cultural contrasts and affinities, making the inevitable losses in translation more perceptible. Paradoxically, this heightened awareness deepens mutual understanding and enriches both versions, fostering a more holistic appreciation of the poetry.

A moktak is a traditional Korean percussion instrument integral to Buddhist ceremonies. Hand-held and often shaped like a fish, this wooden instrument produces a clear, resonant sound when struck. It is used to maintain rhythm during chanting and rituals, guiding the tempo and fostering focus. Its steady, meditative tone makes it an essential tool in Buddhist practices.

작가 소개

양균원(楊均元)

《광주일보》(1981)와 《서정시학》(2004) 시 부문으로 등단. 시집으로 《허공에 줄을 긋다》《딱따구리에게는 두통이 없다》《집밥의 왕자》가 있고 연구서로 《1990년대 미국시의 경향》《욕망의 고삐를 늦추다》 등이 있음. 현 대진대 영문과 교수.

About the Author

Kyoonwon Yang made his literary debut in 1981, winning first prize in the *Kwangju Ilbo* Literary Contest as a third-year college student. After completing military service and graduate studies, he resumed his literary career in 2004 through the literary magazine *Seojeong Sihak*. His poetry collections, published in Korean, include *Drawing Lines in the Void* (2012), *Woodpeckers Don't Get Headaches* (2015), and *The Prince of Home-Cooked Meals* (2020).

In addition to his poetry, Yang has authored critical works in Korean, such as *The Trends of American Poetry in the 1990s* (2011), *Loosening the Reins of Desire* (2014), etc. A dedicated advocate for cross-cultural literary exchange, he has translated and introduced contemporary American and British poets—including recipients of the Pulitzer Prize, National Book Award, and T. S. Eliot Prize—to Korean readers through various literary magazines.

Yang is currently a professor of English at Daejin University, where he teaches modernist and contemporary poetry.

An Ear to Moktak's Knocking
Korean-English Symbiotic Poetry

First Printing, 2025

Published by Sigulli Books
5-1302, Eonjoo-Ro 146-Gil 18, Kangnam-Gu
Seoul 06057, Korea
E-mail: sigulli@naver.com

ISBN: 979-11-990904-0-8 (03810)

₩ 15,000

양균원의 시에는 세심하고 여린 감정의 결이 그대로 살아 있다. 이러한 자신의 감성을 지키기 위함인지 그의 시는 외부세계가 개입하는 것을 끝내 거부하는 포즈를 취하고 있다. 마치 이 시대에 홀로 남은 원시인 같은 얼굴을 한 그의 시의 표정을 살피는 우리의 시선은 자꾸만 감추어진 시인의 내면세계로 향하게 된다.

—이병헌, 《허공에 줄을 긋다》 해설에서

[양균원은] "허기가 깊으면 퍼 올린 국물이 넘치기 마련"인 "세상의 언저리" 어디쯤에서 하명을 기다리는 시종처럼 몽당 연필 한 자루의 형세로 기껍다. 그런 만큼 그의 웃음은 헤프지 않고 그의 다정은 잘 벼려져 있으며, 슬픔조차 단정한 생활의 옷을 입고 있다. 그만큼 진실하다. 떠들썩 갑작스레 좋지는 않지만, 오래 향기를 잃지 않는 힘이 있다.

—이현승, 《딱따구리에게는 두통이 없다》 추천의 글에서

[양균원은] 사라진 것, 흘러간 것, 돌아오지 않는 것들을 호명하면서, 찬(讚)과 탄(歎)과 모(慕)와 경(憬)을 불러 모아 환하게, 여기에, 불빛을 드리워 주는 사람, 나보다 더 나를 아프게 하는 사람, 내 아픔을 나보다 더 사랑하는 사람, 내 사랑보다 더 짙은 사랑의 숲을 가꾸어 놓은 사람, 착하고 맑은 그 사람에게 기댄다.

—장석원, 《집밥의 왕자》 추천의 글에서